Scandinavian Ghost Stories

and

Other Tales of the Supernatural

D1400523

SCANDINAVIAN
Ghost Stories

And Other Tales of the Supernatural

EDITED BY JOANNE ASALA

Penfield
Press

ACKNOWLEDGEMENTS

About the Editor
Joanne Asala is a writer and folklorist living in Chicago, Illinois. Of Finnish and Polish descent, she is the author of over twenty books on folktales and traditional customs including *Trolls Remembering Norway, Norwegian Proverbs, Swedish Proverbs*, and *Proverbs from the North: Words of Wisdom from the Vikings*.

Associate Editors: Miriam Canter, Dorothy Crum, Georgia Heald, Diane Heusinkveld, Joan Liffring-Zug and John Zug

Graphic Design: Robyn B. Loughran

For a complete catalog of titles, please send $2.00 to:
Penfield Press
215 Brown Street
Iowa City, Iowa 52245

For John Zug,
editor and friend

"No man is an island, entire of itself;
every man is a piece of the continent,
a part of the main;
if clod be washed away by sea,
Europe is the less...
any man's death diminishes me,
because I am involved in mankind;
and therefore never send to know
for whom the bell tolls;
it tolls for thee."

— John Donne

INTRODUCTION

Sorcery, witchcraft, magic charms and incantations; graveyards and nocturnal journeys; ghosts, monsters, and demons of the night; the eternal struggle of good versus evil and the quest for ultimate power—these are the themes and elements common to Scandinavian tales of the supernatural.

Open the pages of this book and travel to a frightening world of curses and maleficence, power and greed, and yes, sometimes of hope. These ancient tales from Sweden, Denmark, Norway, Iceland, and Finland can be told on many levels. Some say they are only stories; but the supernatural beings encountered in these tales are creatures of the dark, caricatures of the evil that is in the heart of mankind. The legends warn children to be careful of the hidden dangers of the world, to mind their manners, and to never wander too far from home. Each witch, goblin, or troll may be seen as an undesirable human trait or emotion. Some say the stories are designed for self-reflection, to take notice and correct the hidden qualities within ourselves.

In any case, the telling of such tales is as natural to humans as breathing, and is an on-going part of our culture. Folktales teach us a great deal about past events, superstitions, religious beliefs, social customs and taboos, life-styles and morals. For generations the Scandinavian peasants huddled around their fires, telling tales of the harsh world outside, while they themselves remain safe in their cabins.

So delve into these tales of magic and mayhem, featuring the historic illustrations of such artists as H. J. Ford, and perhaps think with caution the next time you wander out alone at night.

—*Joanne Asala*

TABLE OF CONTENTS

Tales of Wizards and Witches

THE TREASURE-BRINGER

Once upon a time there lived a young farmer named Jaakko Asiainen whose crops had totally failed. His harvest had been spoiled, his hay dried-up, and all his sheep and cattle died, so that he was not able to pay his taxes. One Sunday morning he was sitting at his door, watching the people as they passed by on their way to church. Presently Michel, an old peddler who used to wander about the Finnish countryside, came up his walk. He had a bad reputation. People said that he was a wizard, and an evil one at that. He used to steal the milk from the cows before anyone could milk them. He would call up storms and hail upon the crops, and diseases upon the people, so he was never allowed to leave a farmstead without plenty of gifts.

"Good day, Farmer Jaakko," said Michel when he reached the door.

"God bless you," answered the farmer, eyeing the man cautiously.

"What is it that troubles you?" asked the old man. "You look miserable."

"My life is a mess," sighed Jaakko. "Everything is going badly for me. But now that you're here, it may be that my luck has changed. People say that you have the power to do much evil, but that you are also a clever man. Perhaps you can help me."

"People see evil in others because they themselves are evil," sighed the peddler. "But what can I do? Tell me of your troubles."

Jaakko told him all his misfortunes, and Michel said, "How would you like to escape from all your cares, and to become a rich man at the same time?"

"With all my heart!" cried the other so earnestly that the old man had to smile.

"If I were as young and strong as you, my boy, and if I had enough courage to face the darkness of the night, I know what I would do."

"Tell me what you know!" said Jaakko. "I will do anything if only I can become rich. I am tired of being poor. I always thought I was meant for better things."

Then the old man looked cautiously 'round on all sides, crept closer to the farmer, and said in a whisper, "Do you know what a Kratt is?"

Jaakko was startled, and answered, "I don't know exactly, but I've heard dreadful tales about it. It's an evil creature, a servant of the devil, isn't that right?"

"I'll tell you the truth of it," said the old man. "And mark you, it is a creature that anybody can make for himself. It must be done secretly, however, so that no human eyes can see it. Its body is a broomstick, its head a broken jug, its nose a piece of glass, and its arms two reels which have been used by an old crone of a hundred years. All these things are easy enough to gather, except perhaps for the reels. You must set up this creature on three Thursday evenings at a crossroads, and give it life with the words which I will teach you. On the third Thursday the creature will come to life."

"God preserve us from the evil one!" cried Jaakko in terror.

"What? You are frightened? Foolish man, have I told you too much already? Shall I stop now and go no farther?"

"No, no, I'm not afraid at all," Jaakko insisted. "Go on, please."

The old man continued his tale in a whispery voice, "The Kratt is then your servant, for you have brought him to life at a crossroads. Nobody but you, the master, will be able to see him. He will bring you anything you ask—money, corn, livestock, and hay—as often as you like, but only what an ordinary man can carry at a time."

"But, Michel, if you know all this, why haven't you yourself made such a useful treasure-carrier, instead of living off the charity of others? You can't possibly like being poor, wandering the countryside without a roof of your own."

"I've thought about it a million times, and started the task a thousand times, but my courage always failed me. I had a friend who possessed such a treasure-carrier, and he often told me stories of it. Yet I could not gather enough courage to try it myself."

"Not even the sight of your friend's treasure could persuade you to try?" asked Jaakko.

"My friend died," said the old man simply, "and the creature, left without a master, lived in the village for a long time, bringing about all sorts of mischief. At night he would unravel all of the yarn that the women had spun the day before, or perhaps turn a merchant's stock of wine to vinegar. Eventually a wise woman told the villagers what was happening. They found the place where the creature slept during the day; they smashed the jug head and the glass nose, and broke the broomstick body in two. After this no more was seen of the creature. When I was young, I would have been happy to have a treasure-bringer. But I'm an old man now, and think no more of it. And I'm not ashamed to admit I'm afraid."

"I have plenty of courage," boasted the farmer. "But perhaps I should consult the parson about it first."

"No! You mustn't mention it to anybody, least of all the parson! If you call the creature to life, you sell your soul to the devil!"

Jaakko stared back in horror.

"Don't be frightened," said the old peddler. "You are sure of a long life in exchange, and all that your heart desires. And, if you feel that your last hour is approaching, you can always escape from the clutches of the evil one, if you are clever enough to get rid of your familiar."

"But how can this be done?"

"If you give it a task which it will be unable to perform, you are rid of him for all time. But you must set about it very carefully, for he is not easy to outwit. The friend of whom I told you wanted to get rid of his familiar, and ordered him to fill a barrel of water with a sieve. The creature fetched and spilled water, and did not rest until the barrel was filled with the drops that hung from the mesh."

"So he died without ever getting rid of the Kratt?" asked Jaakko.

"That's the truth of it. Why didn't he manage the affair better? I don't know. It's little enough I have left to tell you, now. The creature must be fed well if he is to be kept in a good mood. A peasant once put a dish of broth under the roof of his familiar, as he always did, but a field worker saw it, and ate the broth and filled the dish with sand. The creature came that night and beat the poor farmer unmercifully, and continued to do so every night until he discovered the reason, and put a fresh dish of broth under the roof. After that he was left alone. So now you know everything there is to know, except the magic words to bring the creature to life."

The farmer sat silently, and at last replied, "There is much about it that is unpleasant, Michel."

"You asked for my advice," answered the old man, "and I have given it to you. You must make your own choice. Want and misery have come upon you. This is the only way in which you can save yourself and become a rich man. If you are only a little prudent, you will cheat the devil out of your soul in the bargain."

After a moment's more consideration, Jaakko said, "Tell me the words which I am to repeat on the Thursdays."

"What will you give me, then?" asked the old man.

"When I have the treasure-bringer, you shall live the life of a gentleman."

"Very well. Come, then," said Michel, and they entered the farmer's cottage together.

After this Sunday, the young farmer was no longer seen in the village. He neglected his work in the fields, and left what little was left to waste, and his household management went astray. His man loafed about the ale houses and his maidservant slept all day. Why should they bother doing any work for a master who did not care to look after anything?

In the meantime, Jaakko sat alone in his smoky room. He kept the door locked and the windows curtained. Here he worked at the Kratt both day and night, the dark room lit only by the light of a pine splinter. He had gathered everything necessary, even the two reels on which a crone of a hundred years had spun. He put all the parts together carefully, fixed the old jug on the broomstick, made the nose of a bit of green bottle glass, and painted in the eyes and red mouth. He wrapped the body in old rags, according to his instructions, and all the time he thought with a shudder that is was now within his power to bring this unnatural creature to life, a creature that would remain with him until the end of his days. When he thought of the riches and treasures, however, his horror vanished.

At last the Kratt was finished, and on the following Thursday, just after nightfall, the farmer carried it to the crossroads in the wood. There he put down the creature, seated himself on a stone, and waited. Every time he looked at the creature, he nearly fainted in terror. Whenever a breeze sprang up, it chilled him to the marrow of his bones. If a screech owl cried from the surrounding forest, he thought it was the croaking of the treasure-bringer, and the blood would freeze in his veins. Morning came at last, and he seized the creature, and scurried quickly home, afraid his neighbors would see him.

On the second Thursday it was just the same.

Finally, the third Thursday came 'round, and Jaakko knew that this was the night he would bring the creature to life. There was a howling wind, and the moon was covered with thick, dark clouds when the farmer brought the creature to the crossroads at dead of night. Then he set it up as before, but he thought, "If I was now to smash this unholy thing into a thousand bits, and go home, and work hard, it need not be said that I did a wicked thing."

Jaakko hesitated for a moment at the crossroads, and said aloud to himself, "But I am so miserably poor, and this will make me rich. The die has been cast, let it go as it may. I won't be worse off than I am now."

He looked fearfully over his shoulder and, trembling, turned toward the creature. He took out his knife, cut the tip of his finger, and let three drops of blood fall on the broken jug head. Then he repeated the magic words which the peddler Michel had taught him.

Suddenly the moon emerged from the clouds and shone upon the place where Jaakko stood with the treasure-carrier. The creature shivered and shook, and the farmer stood petrified with terror as he saw it come to life. The specter rolled his eyes horribly, shook his head as if to wake himself from a deep sleep, and said in a grating voice, "Alive. I am alive." His eyes focused on Jaakko and he growled, "What do you want of me?"

By now the farmer was almost beside himself with fear, and could not find his tongue. He rushed away in deadly terror, not caring where he ran. But the Kratt ran after him, clattering and puffing, crying out all the time, "Why did you bring me to life if you desert me now? Why?"

But the farmer ran on without daring to look behind him.

Then the creature grasped his shoulder from behind with a wooden hand and screamed in Jaakko's ear, "You have broken your compact by running away! You have sold your soul to the dark one without gaining anything. Foolish mortal, you have set me free! I am no longer your servant, but will be your tormentor, your own personal demon, and I will stalk you until your dying hour!"

Jaakko rushed madly to his house, but the creature, invisible to all others, would not leave him alone.

From this hour everything which the farmer undertook went miserably wrong. His land produced nothing but weeds, his remaining cattle died, his sheds fell, and if he picked anything up, even a crock of milk, it broke in his hand. Neither man nor maid would work in his house, and at last all the people stayed clear of his home, just as they would from an evil spirit who brought misfortune wherever he appeared.

Autumn came, and the farmer looked like a shadow of himself. It was then that the peddler Michel returned. "How goes it for you, my good man?" he asked pleasantly.

"Oh, it's you!" cried Jaakko angrily. "It is good that I have met you, you hell hound. Where are all your promises of wealth and good fortune? I have sold myself to the devil, and I find a hell on earth. All this is your doing!"

"Hush! That's enough, now!" said the old peddler. "You dare to blame me? Who told you to meddle with evil things if you had not the courage? I gave you fair warning. It was you who showed yourself to be a coward, and at the last moment it was you who fled and released the Kratt from your service. If you had not done this, you might have become a rich and prosperous man, as I promised."

"You never saw the horrible face of the creature when he came to life," shuddered the farmer. "Oh, what a fool I was to allow myself to be tempted by you!"

"I did not tempt you. I only told you what I knew!" frowned Michel.

"Help me now, please!" begged Jaakko. "There must be something I can do to put an end to this curse!"

"Help yourself, for I can do nothing. Truly, I have more reason to complain than you do. I have not deceived you, I gave you the necessary knowledge and received nothing in return. Where is the reward and the fine life that you promised me? You are the liar, not I."

"Fine, if that's what you want to believe, all right," said Jaakko. "Only, tell me how I can save myself, and I will do anything you ask of me!"

"No," said the old man. "I have no further advice to give you, and wouldn't, even if I knew what to do. I am still a beggar, and it is your fault," and Michel turned around and left the farmer alone.

"Curse upon you!" shouted the farmer, whose last hope was walking down the lane.

"But can't I save myself anyway?" he said to himself. "This creature who sits with the devil on my neck is nothing but my own work—a thing of wood and potsherds. I must be able to destroy him, if I set about it right."

He ran into his house, where he now lived quite alone. The Kratt sat in a corner near the fire, grinning and asking, "Where's my dinner, master?"

"What do you want of me? What must I give you to make you go away?"

"Where's my dinner?" the creature ignored his question. "Get my dinner quickly, Farmer Jaakko, I'm hungry."

Then Jaakko took up a pine torch which was burning in the fireplace and ran out, locking all the doors that led to the outside.

It was a cold autumn night. The wind whistled through the neighboring birch forest with a strange, sighing sound.

"Now you may burn and roast, you spirit of hell!" cried the farmer, and he tossed the torch onto the thatch. At once the entire house was wrapped in bright flames.

Jaakko laughed madly, and he kept calling out, "Burn and roast, you evil demon, burn and roast."

The light of the fire woke up the villagers, and they crowded 'round the cottage. They moved to put out the fire and save the house, but Jaakko pushed them back, saying, "Let it be. Let it burn! What does a house matter, if it means the demon will be dead? He has haunted me long enough, and made my life a hell on earth. I will plague him now, and may yet win."

The people stared at him in amazement as he spoke, sure

that they were hearing the words of a madman. The house fell in upon itself, and the farmer shouted in triumph, "He is finished!"

At that very moment, visible only to the eyes of the farmer, the Kratt rose unharmed from the smoking ruins of the cottage. He grinned horribly at Jaakko, and shook his head. "You will never rid yourself of me, Jaakko Asiainen!" he shouted. "Not in a hundred years!"

When the farmer saw him, he fell on the ground, tearing out his hair and shrieking wordlessly.

"What do you see?" asked Michel, who, like the rest of the villagers, had been roused by the light and smoke. "What is it?"

But the farmer returned no answer. He had died of terror.

LAKE PEIPUS

In former ages, a great and famous king named Krakus ruled over Estonia. In his days, fierce bear and bison lurked in the thick forests, and elk and wild horses ran swiftly through the meadows. No merchants had yet arrived in ships from foreign shores, nor had invading armies conquered with sharp swords to set up the cross of the Christian God, and the people still lived in perfect freedom.

The palace of King Krakus was built of costly sparkling stones and shone in the sun like gold. There the king lived with his court, where his enemies feared him greatly, and his people loved him like a father.

Although the king and queen had gold and honor in abundance, they were lacking one thing to complete their happiness, and that was a child. Now the king lived near the holy forest where dwelt three kind and benevolent gods, and three black-hearted evil ones. King Krakus and his wife prayed to the white gods, promising gifts and sacrifices if they would only listen to their prayers and grant their wish. And lo! After seven years of prayers and sacrifices, the queen gave birth to twins. One was a boy, as bold and impetuous as his father, and one was a girl, with golden hair and eyes like blue cowslips.

The king was filled with joy and made many an offering to the white gods as he had promised. But the black gods, who thought themselves worthy of equal honor, were greatly offended and angry. "How dare King Krakus treat us so!" they muttered to one another. "He will pay for his error, he will pay!" So the black gods went to the God of Death, and begged him to turn his gaze on the king's young son.

"Destroy him!" the evil gods howled. "Make King Krakus pay for daring to ignore us!"

The young prince had been growing rapidly, and was the delight of the entire kingdom; yet, when he came to speak his first words, he was struck cold by Death's evil glance. Before the king and queen's very eyes, their tiny son withered away and died. Rannapuura, the prince's twin sister, lived and flourished like a rose.

The hatred and indignation of the evil gods was not appeased by the partial revenge which they had taken. They gathered together in the shifting shadows of the holy forest and cast dark spells on the Princess Rannapuura.

When the tiny girl was seven years old, she fell into the power of the wicked witch Peipa. The witch snatched Rannapuura from the garden she was playing in, and carried her off to her wretched abode beneath a lofty mountain ridge in Ingermanland. Here the poor child was forced to stay, a servant to Peipa the Witch.

Ten years passed quickly by, and the princess grew into a beautiful maiden despite the hardships she endured. No woman in the world was as fair as she. As the dawn shines ruddy on the borders of the horizon at daybreak, so too shone her hair like red-gold and her cheeks like roses.

King Krakus knew where his daughter was imprisoned, for a good spirit had informed him, but, as mighty as he was, he could not possibly overpower the craft and malice of the witch. He abandoned all hope of ever rescuing his daughter from her rocky prison.

At last the white gods took pity on the royal couple and their daughter. The king, despite the hopelessness in his heart, had continued to pray for aid and offer riches beyond imagine.

Even the gods, however, would not dare to venture into open combat with Peipa. "We must formulate a strategy," each one told the other. "The only way to defeat Peipa is by stealth."

They secretly sent a dove to Rannapuura with a silver comb, a carder, a golden apple, and a snow-white linen cape. They sent, too, a message: "Take the gifts of the white gods and flee from your prison as soon as you can. If Peipa pursues you, call on the white gods and cast one of the objects behind you. Cast first the comb, and if this does not stop her, and she continues to follow you, then throw the carder. If Peipa is not detained and continues to snap at your heels, throw down the apple behind you, and lastly the cape. Be very careful not to make a mistake—be sure to throw down the gifts in the right order."

Rannapuura promised the dove that she would obey the instructions exactly. Then she knelt in prayer to the white gods, thanking them for their kindness, and sent the dove home.

On the first evening after the new moon, Peipa leaped upon her broomstick—as witches are accustomed to do every year on the third, sixth, ninth, and twelfth new moon—and flew away from the house. Rannapuura crept quietly from her room long before the dawn, and took her four gifts of the gods with her on her way. She ran straight toward her father's castle as quickly as she could.

At midday, when she had already gone a good part of the way, Rannapuura chanced to look around, and saw to her horror that the witch Peipa was pursuing her. She rode on a giant rooster, and in her right hand she swung a stout bar of iron.

"Oh good and kindly gods, please help me!" Rannapuura cried, casting the silver comb behind her. Instantly the comb became a rushing river, deep and broad and many miles long. Peipa gazed furiously after the runaway who was traveling swiftly on the opposite bank of the river.

After a time, the witch found a ford through the water, galloped across on her giant rooster, and was soon close behind the maiden again. Now Rannapuura dropped the carder, and lo and behold! A pine forest sprung up, so thick and lofty that the witch and her nightmarish steed could not penetrate it, and were forced to spend the rest of the day riding around it.

Poor Rannapuura had been traveling for two nights and a day without food or rest. Her strength failed her, and on the second day the witch was again close on her heels. Rannapuura threw down the golden apple, crying, "Oh good and kindly gods, please help me!" Instantly the apple became a mountain of granite, with the princess safely on the other side. A narrow path, as if traced by a snake, wound up to the peak and showed the witch the right route. Before she could overcome this obstacle, however, another day had passed.

The princess had only gone a short distance farther, for sleep had at last closed her weary eyes, and when she awoke she could see her father's castle in the distance. The princess rose to her feet, joy leaping in her heart, when she heard a voice behind her screech, "I have you now, my pretty one!" Rannapuura turned to see that the witch was nearly on top of her. There could be no chance of escape! In her terror, she let drop the linen cape from her shoulders. It fell to her feet, and soon rushed forth as a vast and deep lake whose foaming waves raged wildly around the witch. A howling wind swept across the surface, flinging up water and spray into the witch's face. She frantically shouted out spells, but her wickedness could not save her, nor could her steed, the giant rooster. He raised his neck above the water, thrust up his beak, and beat the waves with his wings. Yet it was all to no purpose, and he was drowned.

With prayers and with curses Peipa called on all the spirits of hell to aid her, but none of them appeared, and she sank, howling, into the murky depths. There she lies to this day in pain and torment. The pikes and other horrible creatures of the water gnaw upon her and torture her unceasingly. She strikes about her with her hands and feet, and twists and stretches her limbs in great distress. It is for the witch that the lake received its name, Lake Peipus, and a stormy lake it is.

Rannapuura reached her father's castle in safety, and soon became the bride of a prince. The king's name is still well-known in the church at Krakus, and the estate of Rannapungern, which lies north of Lake Peipus, is named after Rannapuura. The shining waters of the river which rose from the silver comb is known as the River Pliha, and he who knows it now may understand its origins. It cannot run straight, but twists both right and left like the teeth of a double comb, unites with the Narova, and falls with that river into the sea. The forest, too, remained until two-hundred years ago, when the Swedes and the Poles brought war into the land. The Poles concealed themselves in the forest, but the Swedes set fire to it and burned it down. The mountain formed by the golden apple is likewise still standing, but its granite has become changed to sandstone.

THE WITCH IN THE STONE BOAT

There were once a king and a queen, and they had a son called Sigurd who was very strong and brave and handsome. When the king came to be bowed down with the weight of years, he spoke to his son and said, "I think you've reached the age where you should begin to think of taking a wife. I'm not sure how much longer I'll live, and I would like to see you married before I die."

"I've been thinking along those lines myself," said Sigurd. "Where do you think it best for me to look for a wife? Do you have anyone in mind?"

"In the country beyond the mountains there is a princess who is both intelligent and beautiful. I think she would make a perfect bride," said the king. So the two parted, and Sigurd prepared for the journey and went to where his father had directed him.

When Prince Sigurd arrived in the neighboring kingdom, he asked the king for his daughter's hand. This the king agreed to readily, but he added, "You may marry my daughter only on the condition that you should remain here as long as you can, for I myself am not strong and I am no longer able to govern the kingdom."

Sigurd bowed low and said, "I will stay and help you rule your lands, but in the event of my father's death I will have to return to my own country." After that Sigurd married Princess Katarina and helped his father-in-law to govern the kingdom. He and the princess loved each other dearly, and after a year a son was born. When the child was two years old, word came to Sigurd that his father was dead. Sigurd now prepared to return home with his wife and child and went on board the royal ship to go by sea.

They had sailed for several days when the breeze suddenly fell and there came a dead calm over the waters. Sigurd cursed, "We are only a day's journey from my home!"

The calm lasted all through the night and into the next day.

Dawn found Sigurd and his queen on deck when most of the others on the ship had fallen asleep. There they sat and talked for a while, and had their little son along with them. After a time Sigurd became so weary with sleep that he could no longer keep his eyes open; so he went to their cabin to lie down, leaving the queen alone on the deck playing with her son.

A good while after Sigurd had gone below, the queen saw a dark smudge on the sea that seemed to be coming nearer. As it approached, she could make out that it was a boat, and could see the figure of someone sitting and rowing rather quickly. At last the boat came alongside the royal ship, and the queen saw that it was made of stone. An ugly old witch climbed on board. "Good morning, Queen Katarina," she snarled, showing a mouthful of yellowing teeth.

The queen was more frightened than words can describe, and could neither speak nor move from the place to awaken the king or the sailors. The witch came right up to the queen, took the child from her, and laid it on the deck. "Take off your clothes," she demanded. When the queen was stripped of her finery, the witch discarded her own tattered clothes and put on the queen's raiment. Then she seemed to shimmer and waver in the early morning light, until her own form melted away and she became an exact image of the queen. Last of all she picked up the real queen like a sack of potatoes, put her into the boat, and said, "This spell I lay upon you, that your course will not alter until you come to my brother in the underworld."

The queen sat stunned and motionless, and the boat at once shot away from the ship with her. Before long she was out of sight.

When the boat could no longer be seen, the child began to cry, and though the witch tried to quiet him, she could not manage it. She went with the child on her arm to where the king was sleeping, and awakening him, scolded him for leaving them alone on deck while he and all the crew were asleep. "It was careless of you to leave the ship unattended, with only your wife and infant son as guard!"

Sigurd was greatly surprised to hear his queen scold him so much, for she had never said an angry word to him before. He thought it was quite excusable in this case, however, and he tried to quiet the child along with her. But it was no use. Then he went

The Witch comes On board

and wakened the sailors and bade them hoist the sails, for a breeze had sprung up that was blowing straight toward the harbor.

They soon reached the land of Sigurd's birth and found all the people sorrowful for the old king's death. They were glad to have Sigurd back at court, however, and welcomed him as their king.

The king's son had not stopped crying from the time he had been taken from his mother on the deck of the ship, although he had always been such a good child before. At last the king had to get a nurse for him—one of the maids of the court. As soon as the child got into her charge he stopped crying and behaved as well as before.

After the sea voyage it seemed to the king that the queen had changed in many ways, and none of them for the better. He thought her much more haughty and stubborn and difficult to deal with than she used to be.

Before long others began to notice this as well as the king. In the court there were two young fellows, one eighteen years old, the other nineteen. They were very fond of playing chess and often spent whole days playing indoors. Their room was next to the queen's, and sometimes during the day they could hear the queen talking.

One day they paid more attention than usual when they heard her speak, and they put their ears close to a crack in the wall between the rooms, and heard the queen say quite plainly, "When I yawn a little, then I am a nice little maiden; when I yawn halfway, than I am half a troll; and when I yawn fully, then I am a troll altogether."

As she said this she yawned tremendously, and in a moment had put on the appearance of a fearfully ugly troll. Then there came up through the floor of the room a three-headed giant with a trough full of meat, who saluted her and said, "Dear sister, I've brought you your dinner. Are you hungry?"

"Monstrously," she laughed, and began to devour the meat. She never stopped till she had finished it all. The young fellows saw all this going on, but did not hear the two of them say anything to each other. They were astonished, though, at how greedily the queen ate the meat and how much of it she ate.

"I am no longer surprised that she eats so little at the king's table," whispered the elder of the youths.

As soon as the queen had finished, the giant disappeared with the trough by the same way as he had come, and the queen returned to her human shape.

"Should we tell the king of this matter?" whispered the younger of the youths.

"That his wife is a witch? Do you think we'd live to see another sunrise?"

And so the youths decided to keep the story to themselves.

One evening, after the nursemaid had lit a candle and was holding the child, there was a rumble and a roar and several planks sprang up from the floor of the room. Out of the opening came a beautiful woman dressed in white, with an iron belt round her waist to which was fastened an iron chain that went down into the ground. The woman came up to the nurse, took the child from her, and pressed it to her breast. Then she gave it back to the nurse and returned by the same way as she had come, and the floor closed over her again. The woman had not spoken a single word to her, but the nurse was very much frightened and told no one about the incident.

Next evening the same thing happened again, just as before, but as the woman was going away she said in a sad tone, "Two are gone and only one is left." The nurse was still more frightened when she heard the woman say this, and thought that perhaps some danger was hanging over the child, though she had no ill-opinion of the unknown woman, who, indeed, had behaved toward the child as if it had been her own. The most mysterious thing was the woman saying, "and only one is left;" but the nurse guessed that this must mean that only one day was left, since she had come for two days already.

At last the nurse made up her mind to go to the king. "I know it's a strange story," she said. "But you must believe me! Come to the nursery tomorrow, and you will see her."

The king promised to do so, and came to the prince's room and sat down on a chair with his sword in hand. Soon after, there was a rumble and a roar, and the planks in the floor sprang up. The woman in white climbed out with the iron belt wrapped around her waist. The king saw at once that it was his own queen, and immediately hewed asunder the iron chain that was fastened

Sigurd hews the chain asunder.

to the belt. This was followed by such noises and crashing down in the earth that the stone walls of the king's palace shook, so that no one expected anything else than to see every bit of it shaken to pieces. At last the noises and shakings stopped, and they began to come to themselves again.

The king and queen embraced each other, and she told him the whole story—how the witch came to the ship when they were all asleep and sent her off in the boat. "After I had gone so far that I could no longer see the ship, I sailed on through darkness until I landed beside a three-headed giant. The giant wished me to marry him, but I refused, saying I already had a husband. The giant shut me up by myself and told me that I would never get free until I consented to be his wife."

"Oh my poor, dear wife," said King Sigurd, smoothing back his wife's hair. "You were so brave! What happened next?"

"After a time I began to plan how to get my freedom, and at last told the giant that I would consent if he would allow me to visit our son on earth for three final days. This he agreed to, but put on me this iron belt and chain, the other end of which he fastened round his own waist."

"Then the great noises that were heard when I cut the chain must have been caused by the giant's falling down the underground passage!" said the king, hugging his bride close.

"Indeed, the giant's dwelling is right under the palace, and the terrible shakings must have been caused by him in his death throes," said the queen.

The king now understood why the queen had for some time past been so ill-tempered. He at once had a sack drawn over her head and had her tossed into the hole in the floor. She screamed only once, and was heard no more.

The two young fellows now told what they had heard and seen in the queen's room, for before this they had been afraid to say anything about it, because of the queen's power.

The real queen was now restored to all her dignity and was beloved by all. The nurse was married to a nobleman, and the king and queen gave her many splendid presents. And never again were any of them bothered by the creatures of the dark.

THE THREE AUNTS

Once upon a time there was a poor man named Olaf Svenson who lived in a hut in a faraway wood, and he earned his living by hunting. He had lost his wife many years before, and had only one daughter.

When his daughter reached the age of eighteen, she decided it was time to earn her own way in the world. "I don't want to be a burden to you any longer, Father, so I think I will seek employment elsewhere."

"Well, Anna!" said her father. "It's true enough that you have learned nothing here but how to pluck birds and roast them. If your mother had lived she would have taught you to spin and weave and sew; but I could not. What sort of money do you expect to be able to earn? Still, I will let you try to earn your own bread, as is your right."

So the girl went off to seek a place, and when she had gone a little while, she came to a palace. There she stayed and became one of the queen's handmaids. The queen liked her so well that all the other maids grew envious of her. "It's not fair that this strange girl has so quickly become the queen's favorite," said Olga, the leader of the maids.

"I agree," said one of the others. "But what can be done?"

"We must get rid of her," said Olga, "and I know just the way to do it. We will tell the queen Anna has boasted that she can spin a pound of flax in four-and-twenty hours. No one can do that, as you know, and the queen will be so angry with the lie that she will throw Anna out of the castle."

"A marvelous plan!" the others agreed. And so they told the queen just that.

"Have you said this Anna? Then you shall do it," the queen said to the poor girl. "But you may have a little longer time if you choose."

Now, Anna dared not say she had never spun in all her life. She only begged for a room to herself. That she got, and the wheel and the flax were brought up to her. She sat sad and weeping, and did not know what to do. She pulled the wheel this way and that, and twisted and turned it about, but she made a poor hand of it. "How can I possibly spin flax?" she sobbed. "I've never even seen a spinning wheel before!"

As she sat there, an old witch-woman appeared as if from thin air. "What ails you, child?" she asked.

"Ah!" said the poor girl with a deep sigh. "It's no good to tell you, for you'll never be able to help me."

"Who knows?" said the old wife. "I've lived long and seen many things. Maybe I know how to help you after all."

"Well," thought Anna to herself, "I may as well tell her, there's no harm in the telling." So she told her how her fellow-servants had lied and said she could spin a pound of flax in four-and-twenty hours. "And here I am, wretch that I am, shut up to spin all that heap in a day and a night, when I have never even seen a spinning wheel in all my born days."

"Well, never mind that, child," said the old woman. "If you'll call me 'Aunt' on the happiest day of your life, I'll spin this flax for you, and so you may just run along and lie down to sleep."

"Really?" asked Anna, hope stealing into her heart.

"I said I'd do it and so I shall. Now off with you now!" laughed the witch. So Anna went and lay down to sleep.

The next morning when she awoke there lay all the flax spun on the table, and it was so clean and fine that no one had ever seen such even and pretty yarn. The queen was very glad to get such nice yarn, and she set greater store by the girl than ever. But the rest of the handmaids were even more envious. "Let it be agreed that we will tell the queen how Anna had said she was able to weave the yarn she had spun in four-and-twenty hours," said Olga, and this they did.

So the queen said again, "As you said you can do it, Anna, so you must. But if you can't quite finish it in four-and-twenty hours, I won't be too hard upon you, you can take more time."

This time, too, Anna dared not say no, but begged for a room to herself, and then she would try. There she sat again, sobbing and crying, not knowing which way to turn, when another ugly old witch-woman came in and asked, "What ails you, child?"

At first Anna wouldn't say, but at last she told the strange woman the whole story of her grief.

"Well, well!" said the old woman. "Never mind that! If you'll call me 'Aunt' on the happiest day of your life, I'll weave this yarn for you, and so you may just be off, and get some rest. You don't want to ruin your beauty sleep."

The girl agreed, and so she went away and lay down to sleep. When she awoke, there lay the piece of linen on the table, woven so neat and close that no woof could be better. Anna took the fabric and ran down to the queen, who was very glad to get such beautiful linen, and she set greater store than ever by the young girl. But as for the others, they grew still more bitter, and thought of nothing but how to rid themselves of Anna.

"Your highness," Olga approached the queen, "We have heard Anna claim that she can make shirts out of that linen in four-and-twenty hours. Can it be so?"

Well, all happened as before. The girl dared not tell the queen she couldn't sew, and she was shut up again in a room by herself, and there she sat in tears and grief. But then another ugly old witch-woman came in, and she said she would sew the shirts for her if she would call her 'Aunt' on the happiest day of her life. Anna was only too glad to do this, and she went and lay down to sleep.

The next morning when she awoke she found the piece of linen made up into shirts, and such beautiful work no one had ever set eyes on. And more than that, the shirts were all marked and ready for wear. When the queen saw the work, she was so glad at the way in which it was sewn, that she clapped her hands and said, "Such sewing I've never had, nor even seen, in all my born days!" She was as fond of the girl as of her own children, and she said to her, "Now, if you'd like to have the prince for your husband, you shall have him, for you will never need to hire work-women. You can sew, spin, and weave all by yourself."

So as the girl was clever and pretty, the prince was glad to have her, and the wedding took place the very next day. Just as the prince was going to sit down with the bride to the bridal feast, in came an ugly old hag with a long nose—and sure it was at least three feet long!

The bride stood up and made a deep curtsy, saying, "Good-day, Auntie, thank you for coming."

"That woman is aunt to my bride?" the prince gasped in horror.

"Yes, yes she is!" laughed the princess.

"Well, then, she'd better sit down with us to the feast," said the prince, mopping his forehead. But, to tell the truth, both he and the rest of the guests thought she was a loathsome woman to have in their midst.

Just then another ugly old hag came in. She had a back so humped and broad, she had difficulty getting through the door. Up jumped the bride to her feet and called out, "Good-day, Auntie, thank you so much for coming to the feast."

"This w-woman is y-your a-aunt?" stuttered the prince. "Well, she too had better sit down to the feast."

They had scarcely taken their seats before another ugly old hag came in, with eyes as large as saucers that were so red and bleared, 'twas gruesome to look at her. But up jumped the bride again, with her, "Good-day, Auntie," and her, too, the prince asked to sit down. But I can't say he was very glad, for he thought to himself, "Heaven shield me from such aunties as my bride has!"

He could not keep his thoughts to himself any longer, and asked, "My dear Anna, how in all the world can my bride, who is such a lovely girl, have such loathsome, misshapen aunts?"

"I'll soon tell you how it is," said the first witch. "I was just as beautiful as Anna when I was her age, but the reason I've got this long nose is because I was always kept sitting and poking and nodding over my spinning, and so my nose got stretched and stretched until it got as long as you see it now."

"And I," said the second witch, "ever since I was young, have sat and scuttled backwards and forwards over my loom, and that's how my back has got so broad and humped as you now see it."

"And I," said the third, "ever since I was little, I have sat and stared and sewn, and sewn and stared, night and day, and that's why my eyes have got so ugly and red, and now there's no help for them."

"So, so!" said the prince. "'Twas lucky I came to know this, for if folk can get so ugly and loathsome by household work, then my bride shall neither spin, nor weave, nor sew all her life long."

And spin, or weave, or sew the young princess never did.

THE COMPASSIONATE WOODCUTTER

A woodcutter, whose name was Timo Perkkiö, went into the forest one day to chop wood, but each tree begged for mercy in a human voice. "Please, oh please do not chop me down!" each one would plead when they saw the woodcutter approaching with his ax.

"What can I do?" Timo sighed. "How can I continue when you cry with a voice like that of my own children?"

An old man emerged from the thicket. He was just twelve inches high and had a long gray beard, a shirt of birch bark, and a coat of pine bark. He clasped the woodcutter's hands and said, "I am the wizard and guardian of this wood, and I thank you for sparing my children. Because you have been so kind, I will give you this golden rod. It will fulfill all of your wishes."

"All of my wishes, really?" asked Timo.

"Well," the wizard hesitated, "any wish that's not too extravagant as to be impossible."

"Give me an example of a good wish, then," said Timo, "if you don't mind."

And so the woodcutter learned that if he wanted a building erected, he was to bend the golden rod three times toward an ant hill, but not to strike it for fear of hurting the ants. If he wanted food, he must ask the kettle to prepare what he wanted. If it was honey he desired, he must show the rod to the bees, who would then bring him more than he needed. The trees would yield sap, milk, and salve, if he desired it, and if he needed fabrics, the loom would prepare all he needed.

The old man took his leave, and the woodcutter went home to find a quarrelsome wife waiting for him. She scolded him for not bringing any wood, and said, "I wish that all the birch twigs in the forest would turn to rods for the lazy hide!"

"If that is what you wish, Brita Kaisa, let it be so," said the man, and his wife got a sound birching, indeed.

Then he ordered the ants to build him a new storehouse in the yard, and by the next morning it was finished. He now lived

THE WOODCUTTER IN THE TONTLAWALD

a happy life with his wife Brita Kaisa and their children, and at the end of his life he left the rod to his oldest daughter. But in the third generation it fell to a foolish man who began to demand all sorts of absurd and impossible things. At length he shouted to the rod, "It's a chilly day, fetch me the sun and stars from the heavens to warm my back!" Although the sun did not move, God sent down such hot rays from it, that the offender and all his house and goods were burned up. There was no trace of the man at all, and what became of the rod is unknown, but it is thought that the trees in the forest were so terrified by the fire that they have never spoken a word since, but only sigh and rustle to themselves.

THE MAGIC SCYTHE

A certain day-laborer, Jan Fridegård, once left his home in the south of Norway to earn wages for hay-cutting. He traveled to the north country, and there in the mountains he and his horses were suddenly caught in a thick mist and sleet storm and were lost. Afraid to go any further, Jan pitched his tent under an overhanging rock, took out his provisions, and began to eat.

While he was eating, a large brown dog came into the tent, so thin, dirty, wet, and red-eyed that Jan was quite frightened, and gave it as much bread and meat as it wanted. The dog swallowed greedily, and ran off again into the mist and shadows. "Strange it is to see a dog in such a wild and lonely place," the man mused. "One would hardly expect to meet with any living creature here." But after a while he thought no more about the matter. He finished what was left of his supper and quickly fell asleep with his saddle for a pillow.

In the middle of the night, Jan dreamed that he saw a tall and ancient lady enter his tent. She leaned forward and spoke to him in a soft whisper, "I owe you a favor, Jan Fridegård, for your kindness to my daughter, but I'm not able to reward you as you deserve. Here is a scythe which I place beneath your pillow—it is the only gift I can give you. It will no doubt prove useful, for it can cut down all that lies before you. Only beware of putting it into the fire to temper it. Sharpen it however you wish, but never in that way." Without another word, the lady left the tent.

When Jan awoke and looked around, he found that the mist was gone and the sun high in the heavens. He set about gathering his things together, took down his tent, and placed the burden on his pack horses. Last of all he went to saddle his own horse, but when he lifted the saddle from the ground he found beneath it a small scythe-blade that seemed well worn and rather rusty. He at once remembered his dream, and taking the scythe with him, continued on his way. He soon stumbled across the path he had lost, and quickly found his way out of the mountains.

When he arrived in the north country, he went from house to house, but did not find any employment. Every farmer told him the same thing: "You are late, hay-harvest started a week ago, and we have enough laborers."

One farm wife, however, told him of a woman who lived in the area, "She's skilled in magic and very rich, and she always starts her hay-cutting a week later than anybody else."

"Does she have any workers yet?" asked Jan hopefully.

"She rarely hires anybody," the woman admitted, wiping her hands on her apron. "She always seems to manage to get the hay in all by herself. Well, sometimes she does hire a worker, but she's never been known to pay for the work done."

"It doesn't seem like I have much of a choice," sighed Jan. "I must seek this strange woman out." He followed the farm wife's instructions, and soon found himself at the house of the witch.

"I've come to work, if you will have me," said Jan.

"You may work a week for me, but you must not expect any payment," said the witch.

"Those are odd terms, surely, can you explain why they are so?"

"Oh, you will get paid if you can cut more grass in the whole week than I can rake in on the last day of it."

"Really? I'm sure I could do that!" said Jan, feeling much better already.

Jan Fridegård set at once to mowing the old woman's hay. He found that the rusty scythe cut very well indeed and never needed sharpening, even though he used it for five days straight. He was well content, too, with his place, for he found the old woman was kind to him and kept him well fed. There was only one thing that puzzled him. One day, on entering the forge next to the house, he saw a large number of scythe-handles and rakes and a huge pile of blades, and wondered what the old lady could want with all these.

It was the fifth day—the Friday—and when he was asleep that night, the same elf woman whom he had seen in the mountains came again to him and said, "Large as the meadows are that you have mown, your employer will easily be able to rake in all that hay tomorrow, and if she does so, she will—as you know—drive you away without paying you."

"What can I do?" asked Jan. "Has all of my work been for nothing?"

"When you see yourself bettered by the old woman, go into the forge and take as many scythe handles as you think you can carry, fit their blades to them, and carry them out to the part of the land where the hay is yet uncut. There you must lay the blades on the ground, and you shall see how things go."

This said, the elf woman disappeared, and in the morning Jan, getting up, set to work as usual at his mowing. At six o'clock the old witch came out, carrying five rakes with her, and said to the man, "It's a fine piece of ground you've mowed, indeed!" She spread the rakes upon the hay. Then the man saw, to his astonishment, that though the one she held in her hand raked in great quantities of hay, the other four raked in no less, each on its own accord, and with no hand to wield it.

At noon, seeing that the old woman would soon get the best of him, he went into the forge and took out several scythe handles, attached their blades, and brought them out to the field. There he laid them on the ground near the grass that still needed cutting. All the scythes set to work on their own accord, and cut down the grass so quickly that the rakes could not keep pace with them. And so they went on all the rest of the day, and the old woman was unable to rake in all the hay that lay in the fields. After dark she told him to gather up his scythes and take them into the house again, while she collected her rakes. "You are wiser than I took you to be, my boy. You know more than myself, so much the better for you, for you may stay as long as you like with me."

So Jan spent the entire summer in the witch's employment, and they got along very well together, mowing with very little trouble a vast amount of hay. In the autumn she sent him away, well laden with money, to his own home in the south. Next summer, and more than one summer following, Jan worked in her employ, always being paid as much as his heart desired at the end of the season.

After some years, he bought a farm of his own in the south country, and was always seen by his neighbors as an honest man, a good fisherman, and an able workman in whatever work he might put his hand to. He always cut his own hay, never using any scythe but that which the elf woman had given him upon the mountains; nor did any of his neighbors ever finish their mowing before him.

One summer it happened that while he was out fishing, one of his neighbors came to his house and asked his wife to lend him her husband's scythe, as he had lost his own. The farmer's wife looked for one, but could only find the one upon which her husband set such store. She lent this to the man, a little afraid, begging him at the same time to never temper it in fire, for that, she said, her good husband never did.

So the neighbor promised, and taking it with him, bound it to the handle and began to work with it. But sweep as he would and strain as he might (and sweep and strain he did rather well) not a single blade of grass fell. The man tried to sharpen it, but with no luck. Then he took it into the forge, intending to temper it, for, thought he, what harm could that possibly do? But as soon as the flames touched the blade it melted like wax, and nothing was left of it but a little heap of ashes. Seeing this, he went in haste to Jan's house, and told the woman what had happened. She was at her wits' end with fright and shame when she heard it, for she knew well enough how her husband set store by his scythe, and how angry he would be at its loss.

And angry he was when he came home, and he yelled and hollered at his wife for her folly. "Kristina, how can you lend out something that is not yours to lend?" But seeing how his words affected her so, he sighed and finally said, "Long have I depended on this gift of magic, but even longer did I have no magic to work with at all. I think, then, that it's time to return to my prior ways. The loss of the scythe, after all, is not really so terrible."

The farmer was still the hardest working man in the district, and prospered for many years after.

THE WITCH THORBJÖRG

'Twas in the faraway of long ago, when the world was rarer and happenings stranger, that a great famine swept through Greenland. Those who had been fishing had but small catches, and some had not returned at all from the sea.

There was a woman of Greenland who lived in the district of Thorbjörg, and she was a *spœwife* (fortune teller) known as the Little Witch. She had nine sisters, all of them witches, but she was the only one to have survived the famines. It was her habit in the wintertime to go to the various feasts, and many men invited her to sit with them, especially those who were curious to know their fortunes and what the future would hold.

At one particular feast it was decided that Thorkell, the leading man, would ask the one question that plagued all of their minds: When would the famine end? Thorkell therefore invited the *spœwife* to his house, and a good reception was prepared for her, as was the custom when such distinguished women were to be received. A high, comfortable seat was made ready for her, with a thick cushion stuffed with hens' feathers.

When she arrived, she was dressed like a princess, and had over her a blue cloak with straps that were set with stones right down to the bottom. On her neck she had glass beads, and on her head a black cap of lambskin lined with white catskin. In her hand she carried a staff with a knob on it that was mounted with brass and set with costly stones. About her waist she wore a tinder belt, and on it a great skin-purse in which she kept the charms that she required to gain knowledge of anything. She had shaggy calfskin shoes on her feet, and in these were long and stout thongs with large knobs of brass at the ends. On her hands she wore catskin gloves that were white and furry inside.

When she entered, it was thought every man's duty to give her honorable greetings, which she received according to the liking she had for each. Thorkell then took the hand of the wisewoman and led her to the seat that was prepared for her.

"Take a look at my cattle, household, and homestead! I'm sure you'll find it a fine place!" he boasted rather loudly. The witch-woman, however, seemed unusually reserved about everything. Tables were laid, and the food that was served to the *spæwife* could not be rivaled. For her was made porridge with kid's milk, and for meat were prepared the hearts of every kind of animal that could be got. She had a brass spoon and an ivory-handled knife with two rings of brass on it, but the point of it was broken.

When the feast was ended and the tables were cleared away, Thorkell came before Thorbjörg and asked what she thought of his homestead and his people. "How quickly can you get the answers to any question I give you?" he asked.

"I will not disclose any answers until the morning," said Thorbjörg solemnly, "not until after I've slept through the night."

"I suppose I will have to wait then," sighed Thorkell.

The next morning she was supplied with all that she required to perform her enchantments, and said, "Summon for me the Vardlokkur, the woman of your household who knows the charms that are necessary to perform the enchantment."

A search was made through the entire household to find someone who knew of such a woman. Unfortunately, no one knew where a Vardlokkur could be found. Then a woman named Gudrid answered, "I am neither witch nor wise woman, yet my mother, who lived in Iceland, taught me the charm she called Vardlokkur."

"Then you are learned in season," said Thorbjörg.

"This is a learning and proceeding of such a kind as I mean to take no part in!" insisted Gudrid. "I am a Christian woman."

"It might well be that you could help people in this matter," said Thorbjörg. "I do not think you would be worse a woman than before. But I leave it to Thorkell to provide all that is needed here. It does not matter to me."

Thorkell now pressed hard until Gudrid consented to do as he wished. The other women made a ring round the Vardlokkur while Thorbjörg sat on the spell-seat. Then Gudrid sang the spell-song so beautifully that all who were present thought they had never heard a voice sing more sweetly. The *spæwife,* with tears in her eyes, thanked Gudrid for her song, and added, "Many spirits have come here, spirits who formerly would turn away from us and show us no obedience. They thought what was sung was beautiful. Now many things are made clear to me that before this were concealed both from me and from others. I can now tell you this, that the famine will not last much longer, and the season will improve with the coming of spring."

Tales of Ghosts, Specters, and Spirits

A Tale of Vengeance

Once upon a time, and a good time it was, two friends spent the night before a roaring fire, conversing together on various subjects, and, among others, on corpses.

"If ever I happen to find a dead man," said the one, "I shall do my best for it, and bury it. There's an old Viking saying that demands, 'Bury the bodies of the fallen when you find them in your travels, whether they be killed by disease or drowned in the sea or slain on the field of battle.'"

"As if you've ever met a Viking!" scoffed the other. "For my part, I shall take no such trouble, but pass it by like any other carrion. Why should I wear myself out on someone I don't know?"

Some time passed away, and one day Ketill—that was the name of the second young man—while out walking, found the body of an old woman lying in the road. But he stepped over it without paying it a second glance.

The very next night, after he was in bed, this same old woman appeared to him and hissed, "No thanks to you, Ketill, for your cruel neglect of me! You did me neither good nor evil."

She looked so horrible that the man jumped out of bed, grabbed a large knife that he kept under his pillow, and chased the ghost from the house, cursing and shouting and crying, "Shall I stab you, you old witch, you?" Feeling quite confident, he went back to bed and quickly fell asleep.

The man again woke with a start to find the ghost in his room, holding her bloody lungs in her hand and gesturing as if she would strike him with them. "Did I not teach you the first time?" the man asked. "Get out of my house!" He reached under the pillow to grab his knife, but the woman vanished once more.

When he had gone to bed again and was asleep, although this time it took him much longer to relax, the ghost of the old woman came a third time and reached her long, bony hands toward his neck as if she would choke the very life out of him. A third time he leaped out of bed with the knife, and a third time the old woman vanished.

The hag's ghost followed the unhappy Ketill all his life, and drove him with her wrath and spite into an untimely grave. Whether Ketill's friend ever found a corpse and had a chance of carrying out his charitable intentions with regard to it, this story narrates not; neither does it so much as hint at what reward he would have gotten for his pains.

JØRGEN AND HIS DEAD MASTER

Jørgen Sørensen was a bit of a lady's man who was very fond of amusing himself with the village girls, and often sat up talking and joking with them till very late in the evening. One Sunday, when he had slept very little the night before, he went to church, and there he fell asleep and did not awake till dark night. He rubbed his eyes and could not imagine where he was, for the church was full of people, and they were all fine gentlemen. Jørgen looked about and recognized among them his former master, who had been buried the previous spring. His former master asked, "Well, Jørgen, when did you die?"

"Three months after you were buried," answered Jørgen.

"Oh, indeed," said the gentleman. "But what do you think? Should we have a little fun? Let's go home now for a short visit. Won't you accompany me?"

"I'm ready," said Jørgen, and he rose and followed his master. On the way he found a frozen glove, which he put in his pocket. They came to the mansion, and the master went first to the stable, for he intended to torment the horses and thought Jørgen would help him.

When the gentleman entered, the horses made no sound, but when Jørgen came in through the door they neighed and bucked. The master turned around and said, "Listen, Jørgen! Is this a trick? You can't really be dead. Give me your hand to feel." Jørgen thrust his hand into the frozen glove which he had found on the road, and extended it to his master, who said, "Yes, you are really dead. Your hand is shockingly cold." Then he tormented the poor horses till they were covered with white foam. Jørgen was sorry, but could do nothing but stand and look on.

At last the master ceased his spiteful work, and said, "Let us go into the house. You go into the kitchen and frighten the maids, and I will torment my old wife. When it is time to go, I will come for you." The lady of the house screamed and sobbed with terror as if she were going mad, and the maids screamed too, but with fun and frolic.

After a long time, the master came to the kitchen, and said, "Come, Jørgen, we have to hurry, for the cocks will soon crow." Jørgen would have liked to run away, but he was too much afraid of his master's ghost, so he went along. On the way his master talked a great deal to him about how his wife had searched everywhere for the treasure that he had hidden before his death, and what she had done to banish the nightly haunting, and that everything was useless.

"Yes," said Jørgen, "it must be a great sorcerer who can lay specters in their grave and discover treasures in the ground. Perhaps she will never meet with one."

"Ha! Ha!" laughed the gentleman. "It's obvious you're still new to all this. No great cleverness is needed. If a living person were to stamp three times on my grave with his left heel and say each time, 'Here shall you lie,' I couldn't get out again. And the money which I hid in my lifetime is closer than my widow thinks; it is under the floor of my bedroom, near the stove."

Jørgen was delighted to hear this, and would have shouted for joy but thought it too dangerous.

They now came to the churchyard, and the gentleman asked Jørgen to show him his grave. But Jørgen said, "We shall have another opportunity tomorrow night; I'm afraid the cocks are just about to crow."

"Quite right," the gentleman said as he slipped quickly into his grave.

Jørgen stamped three times with his left heel on the mound, and said three times, "Here shall you lie! Here shall you lie! Here shall you lie!"

"Oh, you liar and scoundrel!" cried the dead man from the grave. "If I had known that you were still alive, I would have crushed and mangled you. Now I can do nothing more to you."

Jørgen returned home full of joy, and told the lady all that he had seen and heard and done. The lady did not know how to thank him enough. She took him as her husband, and they lived together happily and honorably, and if they could have gotten on as well with Death as with the nocturnal specter, they might be living still.

Murder Will Out

Once upon a time, in a certain churchyard outside of Copenhagen, some people who were digging a grave found a skull with a knitting pin stuck through it from temple to temple. The priest took the skull and kept it hidden until the next Sunday when he had to perform service.

When the day came, the priest waited until all the people were inside the church, and then fastened the skull above the doorway. After the service the priest and his servant left the church first, and stood outside, carefully watching everybody that came out. When all the congregation had passed out without anything strange occurring, they looked in to see if there was anyone still remaining inside. The only person they saw was a very old woman sitting behind the door, who was so unwilling to leave the church that they had to force her out. As she passed under the porch, three drops of blood fell from the skull onto her white headdress, and she exclaimed, "Alas! Murder will out at last!" Then she confessed that having been forced to marry her first husband against her will, she had killed him with a knitting-pin and married another.

THE GHOST'S QUESTIONS

One time a young woman named Riita was walking home from her grandfather's house on the path that led past the cemetery in Toholampi. Passing by a rather large and imposing gravestone, she heard a dim and ghostly voice ask, "What is your name, my girl? Whose daughter are you? Where do you come from? Where are you going? And how many nights old is the moon?"

The girl, tired from the long day and in no mood to stand around chatting with a ghost, answered quickly, "My name is Riita Erkintytar. My father's name is Erik Paavonpoika and my mother Anni Mikontytar. I'm coming from my grandfather's and I'm going home to cook supper for my children. And the moon," she finished, "is six days old. Are there any other questions?"

All Riita heard, however, was a faint rustling sound. It could have been the wind blowing through the trees, or it could have been a ghostly murmuring. Who's to say? But it is well-known in Toholampi that if Riita had stumbled over any of her answers, the ghost would have gotten power over her.

THORGILS OF FLÓI AND THE HOUSEHOLD GHOSTS

Thorgils was born in Flói, which is in the southwest part of Iceland, and at the age of sixteen he decided to leave his home and travel to Norway. This move greatly angered Gunnhild, the king of Iceland's mother, because she wished him to stay and become a retainer to her son.

Despite her anger, the king's mother could not stop Thorgils from joining a merchant vessel, and in the autumn of that year he found himself in the south of Norway. There he took up lodging with a widow and her son, who was named Audun. The widow was gifted in the magical arts, and she treated Thorgils with great kindness and hospitality. Yet it was not long before Thorgils left and moved into the house of a man named Björn, where he was also well-received.

This particular household always went to bed early, and Thorgils asked, "What is the reason for this? Hardly has the sun slipped below the horizon; there are many more hours left before one should have to retire."

Björn sighed and a weariness seemed to come over him, "I know it must seem strange to one so young and full of life, but my reasoning is this. My father, who has only recently died, is not at rest and his ghost walks up and down the halls of my home, frightening all who encounter him. It is to avoid such trials that we go to sleep early."

Often during the winter months, Thorgils heard something scurrying across the roof and hammering at the windows. One night, although he knew it would no doubt anger his host, he rose from bed and went outside, ax in hand. Before the door stood a ghost, just as if he had been waiting for him. The youth wrinkled his nose in disgust, for the ghost smelled both sweet and rotten, like cut hay left too long in the corner of the barn. Thorgils raised the ax, but the ghost turned away. He floated several yards down the path and then turned, beckoning Thorgils to follow. Thorgils lay the ax across his shoulder, "As if it would've done me any good against a ghost!"

The ghost led the youth toward a burial mound. "Is this where your body lies?" Thorgils asked. "Why are you not at rest?"

Instead of answering him, the ghost turned and struck him across the face. Thorgils stumbled, dropping the ax. "I thought that ghosts were incapable of hurting people!" he shouted. "You're not supposed to be made of real matter!"

"You thought wrong!" laughed the ghost, striking him again. They wrestled with each other, and the struggle was both hard and fierce, so that the very earth was torn up by their feet. But the fates were smiling on Thorgils that night, and in the end it was the ghost who fell flat on his back. Thorgils hovered above him. Managing to reach his ax, he took a deep breath, swung the glinting blade high into the air and brought it hurtling back down. The ax clanged on the stony ground and the ghost's head went twisting and bouncing from his body.

The ghost's head looked around in shock, but before it could speak Thorgils said, "I do not want you to bother Björn, or anyone else in his household, again. Do I make myself clear?" The ghost could only blink in acceptance before both the head and the body faded away in the gray light of dawn.

Björn, of course, was pleased with the young man, and praised him highly in front of the entire household. Everyone thought their ghostly troubles were over.

Yet one night a knock came to the door. Thorgils went outside and there found his old friend Audun looking pale and shaky. "What is it, my friend? What has happened to bring you out in the middle of the night?"

"It's my mother," Audun wept, "Gyda has died this evening, but I believe there is something strange about her death."

"Strange? How so?" asked Thorgils.

"I can't say, really, or rather, I don't wish to discuss it at the moment. All the men in our household have run away; no one dared to stay and keep the wake with me. Now I want to bury her, and I ask you to come help me."

"Gladly," said Thorgils. "Lead on." He did not think to inform Björn about what was happening, and he followed his friend out into the darkness without another word.

When they reached the farm, Audun said, "Thorgils, I want you to build a coffin for my mother with a hearse beneath it. Make sure you fix strong clasps on it, for we don't want any risk of it opening."

"Opening? How would it open?" Thorgils asked, but his friend averted his eyes and would say nothing.

When all this was done, Audun said, "And now we must take it away and bury it, and pile as much earth and stone on it as we can." So they set out with it, but before they had gone far the coffin began to creak loudly and one by one the clasps snapped apart. The lid tumbled aside and the corpse of Gyda sat up. It took all of the strength of the two men to get her back into her coffin. "We'll have to change our plans," said Audun. "I think her body should be cremated instead."

"I think I agree," said Thorgils shakily. They carried her to a funeral pile which Audun had prepared; on this they placed the body of the old woman and set fire to the casket and hearse. Then they stood by to ensure it was burned through and through. "Great friendship have you shown me this night, Thorgils, and manly courage. I can't thank you enough."

"There is no need to, Audun. I respected your mother and would not want to see her wraith walking through the countryside."

"Still, I shall give you a new sword and a kirtle, but if I ever ask for the sword back, I wish you to let me have it and I shall give you another weapon just as good." With this they parted ways, and Thorgils went back to the home of Björn, who had been bemoaning the fact that his favorite man had been snatched away by trolls or evil spirits.

"Again you have kept a ghostly creature from haunting the neighborhood," said Björn, "and we shall drink to your bravery and courage." Many days of feasting followed, and never again did ghosts haunt the homestead of Björn.

THE SPIRITS OF
THE NORTHERN LIGHTS

A certain nobleman was in the habit of driving away from his mansion every evening during hard winters, and not returning till the first light of dawn. He had strictly forbidden any of his people to accompany him, or to receive him on his return. He harnessed the horse to the sledge himself, and unharnessed him when he returned. No one was permitted to see the horse and carriage, and he threatened everyone with death should they venture into his secret stable in the evening. During the day he carried the stable key in his pocket, and at night he hid it under his pillow.

But the nobleman's coachman was much too anxious to know where his master went every evening, and he wished to know what the horse and carriage were like. So one day he picked the lock to the stable and hid himself in a dark corner near the door.

He didn't have to wait long before his master came and opened the door. All at once the stable shone as if a hundred candles had been lit. The coachman crouched in his corner like a hedgehog, knowing that if his master saw him he would certainly suffer the threatened punishment.

The master pushed the sledge forward, and it shone like a red-hot anvil. When he went to fetch the horse, the coachman crept under the sledge.

The nobleman harnessed the horse, and threw heavy cloths over both horse and sledge so that the people about the yard should not see the wonderful radiance.

The coachman crept quietly from under the sledge and hid himself behind on the runners, where by good luck his master did not notice him.

When all was ready, the nobleman sprang into the sledge, and they went off so rapidly that the runners of the sledge resounded in the cold night air. They always headed due north, and after some hours the coachman saw that the cloths were gone from the horse and sledge. Again it shone like fire.

Now, too, he saw that ladies and gentlemen were driving up from all directions with similar sledges and horses. That was a rush and a rattle! The drivers raced past each other as though it was for a very heavy wager, or as if they were on their wedding journey. At last the coachman saw that their course lay above the clouds, which stretched below them like smooth lakes.

After a time, the racers fell more and more behind, and the coachman's master said to his nearest companion, "Brother, the other spirits of the Northern Lights are departing. Let us go too!"

Then the master and coachman drove home fast. The next day people said they had never seen the Northern Lights so bright as the night before.

The coachman held his tongue, and trusted no one with the story of his nocturnal journey. But when he was old and gray he told the story to his grandson, and so it became known to the people. And it was said that such spirits still exist, and that when the Northern Lights flame in the heavens in winter they hold a wedding in the sky.

THE SPIRIT OF THE WHIRLWIND

Two men were walking together one blustery day when they saw a haystack carried away by the wind. The elder man said it was the Spirit of the Whirlwind, but the other would not believe him till they saw a cloud of dust.

"Turn around quickly," said the older of the two, and they turned their backs to the dust cloud. The young man repeated a spell after the old one, and when they turned back around, they saw an old gray man with a long white beard, a broad flapping coat, and streaming hair, tearing the trees from their roots.

The wild spirit took no notice of them, but the elder man cautioned the other not to forget to repeat the spell whenever he saw the dust cloud. The youth forgot it, however, and the whirlwind in a fury carried him many miles from home, and ever afterward tossed him about till he went to his friend and learned the spell again.

The next time he saw the whirlwind he was fishing, and on his repeating the spell, the spirit passed him angrily, and a great wave surged up from the river and wetted the man to the skin. But after that the spirit never reappeared to him, and left him in peace.

THE WILL O' THE WISPS

A farmer named Per was driving home one winter evening from Fellin across the Parika heath, when he suddenly saw a little blue flame on one side, and his horse stopped short and would not move. It was as if he had been stopped by a ditch. He dismounted, and found not a ditch, but an open pit. He could not drive around it because there was deep water on all sides. Presently he saw a light flare up like a torch, and then another, till many of them were flitting about everywhere.

In consternation, the farmer cried out, "Father, Son, and Holy Ghost, what's going on here tonight?" The horse sprang forward as if somebody had stuck a pin into him, and the farmer had only just time to tumble on the sledge, when they went off at full gallop. The mysterious pit had disappeared. Afterward the farmer could only say that the name of God had occurred to him just at the right time.

THE NOCTURNAL CHURCH-GOERS

One Christmas Eve the people at a farmhouse a couple of miles from the church in Vasa went to bed shortly after supper, intending to go to the early morning service by candlelight. The farmer woke up, and on going out to see how the weather was saw the church lit up. Thinking that he had overslept, he called his family and they set out. They found the church lit up and full of people, but the singing sounded rather strange. When they reached the open door, the lights and people disappeared and a stranger came out. The man, whose face was hidden by a dark hood, said, "Return home. This is our service. Yours begins tomorrow." He took one of the farmer's sons aside and told him to come again at midnight three days before St. John's Eve and he would make his fortune. "But you must keep it a secret," he warned.

As the party returned to the farmhouse, the sky cleared and they saw from the position of the stars that it was midnight. When the matter came to the pastor's ears, he tried to persuade the people that it was only a dream; but the incident could not be hushed up.

The youth who had received an invitation from the stranger felt very doubtful about keeping the appointment, especially as he had been commanded to keep it secret. But a fortnight before the time, as he was going home one evening after sunset, he saw an old woman sitting by the roadside, who asked him what he was thinking about so deeply.

He didn't answer, and then she said, "Let me see your hand, Theodor, so that I might tell your fortune." She put on her glasses and, after examining his hand for some time, promised him good fortune, and told him, "Go with the stranger without fear. You have nothing to worry about."

"What else do you see?" he asked, his curiosity getting the better of him.

"Nothing else but this: If you wish to take a wife, do so only with great consideration, or you might fall into misfortune." She refused any payment, and hurried away as lightly as a young girl.

Three days before St. John's Eve, Theodor set out a little before midnight. A voice cried in his ear, "You are not going right!" He was about to turn back when he heard other voices singing in the air, "Do not throw away such good fortune. Proceed, proceed!"

The youth found the church door closed, but the hooded stranger came from behind the left side of the church and said, "I feared that you might not have come."

"I almost didn't," Theodor admitted.

The stranger then told the farmer's son that there was a grave mound in a certain meadow behind the church. "Three juniper bushes grow on it," he said, "and under the middle one a great treasure is buried. In order to appease the guardians of the treasure, it is necessary to slaughter three black animals—one feathered and two hairy—and to take care that not a drop of the sacrificial blood is lost. A bit of silver should be scraped from your buckle so that the gleam of the costly silver might lead you to that which is buried. Then cut a stick from the juniper three spans long, turn the point three times toward the grass where you have offered the blood, and walk nine times around the juniper bush from west to east. At every round strike the grass under the bush three times with the stick, and at every blow say, 'Igrek!' At the eighth round you will hear a jingling of money, and after the ninth round you will see the gleam of silver. Then fall on your knees, bend your face to the ground and cry out nine times, 'Igrek!' The treasure will rise. You must wait patiently till the treasure has risen, and not allow yourself to be frightened by the specters which will appear, for they are only soulless phantoms trying to steal your courage. If it fails, you will return home with empty hands."

"Why must I go on St. John's Eve?"

"That is when the bonfires are burning and the people are merrymaking. It is a magic time."

"I will be rich!" shouted Theodor.

"As to the treasure," the stranger interrupted, "a third should be given to the poor, the rest belongs to the finder."

The stranger repeated his directions three times word for word so that the farmer's son should not forget them. When the sexton's cock crew, the stranger vanished suddenly without another word.

The next day the youth obtained a black cock and a black dog from the neighbors, and later that night he caught a mole. On St. John's Eve he took the three animals and carried out his instructions at midnight, slaughtering first the cock, then the mole, and lastly the dog, taking care that every drop of blood should fall on the appointed spot. When he called "Igrek!" at the conclusion of the ceremony, a fiery-red cock rose suddenly under the juniper, flapped its wings, crowed, and flew away. A shovel full of silver was cast up at the youth's feet. Next a fiery-red cat with long golden claws rose from under the juniper, mewed, and darted away, and the earth opened some more and threw up another shovel full of silver. Next appeared a great fiery-red dog with a golden head and tail, who barked and ran away, and another shovel full of silver coins was cast up at Theodor's feet. This was followed by a red fox with a golden tail, a red wolf with two golden heads, and a red bear with three golden heads. Behind each animal money was thrown out on the grass, but behind the bear there came a ton of silver, and the entire heap rose to the height of a haycock. When the bear disappeared, there was a rushing and roaring under the juniper as if fifty smiths were blowing the bellows at once. Then appeared from the juniper a huge head, half-man and half-beast, with golden horns nine feet long, and with golden tusks two ells long. Still more dreadful were the flames which shot from mouth and nostrils, and which caused the rushing and roaring. The youth was now beside himself with terror, and rushed away, fancying himself closely pursued by the specter, and at last he fell down in his own farmyard and fainted. In the morning the sunbeams roused him, and when he came to himself he took six sacks with him from the barn to carry off the treasure. He found the hill with three junipers, the slaughtered animals, and the wand, but the earth showed no signs of having been disturbed, and the treasure had vanished. Probably it still rests beneath the hill, waiting for a bolder man to raise it.

Had the man been equally unfortunate in the subject of his marriage? Unfortunately this storyteller does not know.

Tales of Monsters

THE TERRIBLE OLLI

There was once a wicked, rich, old troll who lived on a mountain that sloped down to a bay. A decent Finn, a farmer, lived on the opposite side of the bay. The farmer had three sons. When the boys had reached manhood he said to them one day, "I should think it would shame you three strong youths that the wicked old troll over there should live on year after year and no one trouble him. We work hard like honest Finns and are as poor at the end of the year as at the beginning. That old troll with all his wickedness grows richer and richer. I tell you, if you boys had any real spirit you'd take his riches from him and drive him away!"

His youngest son, whose name was Olli, at once cried out, "Very well, Father, I will!"

But the two older sons, offended at Olli's promptness, declared, "You'll do no such thing! Don't forget your place in the family! You're the youngest and we're not going to let you push us aside. Now, Father, we two will go across the bay and rout out that old troll. Olli may come with us if he likes and watch us while we do it."

Olli laughed and said, "All right!" for he was used to his brothers treating him like a baby.

So in a few days the three brothers walked around the bay and up the mountain to the troll's house. The troll and his old wife were both at home. They received the brothers with great civility.

"You're the sons of the Finn who lives across the bay, aren't you?" the troll asked. "I've watched you boys grow up. I am certainly glad to see you for I have three daughters who need husbands. Marry my daughters and you'll inherit my riches." The old troll made this offer in order to get the young men into his power.

"Be careful," Olli whispered.

But the brothers were too delighted at the prospect of inheriting the troll's riches so easily to pay any heed to Olli's warning. Instead they accepted the troll's offer at once.

Well, the old troll's wife made them a fine supper and after supper the troll sent them to bed with his three daughters. But first he put red caps on the three youths and white caps on the three troll girls. He made a joke about the caps. "A red cap and a white cap in each bed!" he said.

The older brothers suspected nothing and soon fell asleep. Olli, too, pretended to fall asleep, and when he was sure that none of the troll girls was still awake he got up and quietly changed the caps. He put the white caps on himself and his brothers and the red caps on the troll girls. Then he crept back to bed and waited.

Presently the old troll came over to the beds with a long knife in his hand. There was so little light in the room that he couldn't see the faces of the sleepers, but it was easy enough to distinguish the white caps from the red caps. With three swift blows he cut off the heads under the red caps, thinking of course they were the heads of the three Finnish youths. Then he went back to bed with the old troll wife, and Olli could hear them both chuckling and laughing. After a time they went soundly to sleep as Olli could tell from their deep regular breathing and their loud snores.

Olli now roused his brothers and told them what had happened, and the three of them slipped quietly out of the troll house and hurried home to their father on the other side of the bay.

After that the older brothers no longer talked of robbing the troll of his riches. They didn't care to try another encounter with him.

"He might have cut our heads off!" they said, shuddering to think of the awful risk they had run.

Olli laughed at them.

"Come on!" he kept saying to them day after day. "Let's go across the bay to the troll's!"

"We'll do no such thing!" they told him. "And you wouldn't suggest it either if you weren't so young and foolish!"

"Well," Olli announced at last, "if you won't come with me I'm going alone. I've heard that the troll has a horse with hairs of gold and silver. I've decided I want that horse."

"Olli," his father said, "I don't believe you ought to go. You know what your brothers say. That old troll is an awfully sly one!"

But Olli only laughed. "Good-bye!" he called back as he waved his hand. "When you see me again I'll be riding the troll's horse!"

The troll wasn't at home but the old troll wife was there. When she saw Olli she thought to herself, "Mercy me, here's that Finnish boy again, the one that changed the caps! What shall I do? I must keep him here on some pretext or other until my husband comes home!"

So she pretended to be very glad to see him. "Why, Olli," she said, "is that you? Come right in!"

She talked to him as long as she could and when she could think of nothing more to say she asked him, "Would you take the horse and water it at the lake?"

"That will keep him busy," she thought to herself, "and long before he gets back from the lake the troll will be here."

But Olli, instead of leading the horse down to the lake, jumped on its back and galloped away. By the time the troll reached home, he was safely on the other side of the bay.

When the troll heard from the old troll wife what had happened, he went down to the shore and hallooed across the bay, "Olli! Oh, Olli, are you there?"

Olli made a trumpet of his hands and called back, "Yes, I'm here! What do you want?"

"Olli, have you got my horse?"

"Yes, I've got your horse, but it's my horse now!"

"Olli, Olli!" his father cried. "You mustn't talk that way to the troll! You'll make him angry!" And his brothers looking with envy at the horse with gold and silver hairs warned him sourly, "You better be careful, young man, or the troll will get you yet!"

A few days later Olli announced, "I think I'll go over and get the troll's money bag."

His father tried to dissuade him, "Don't be so foolhardy, Olli! Your brothers say you had better not go to the troll's house again."

But Olli only laughed and started gaily off as though he had not a fear in the world.

Again he found the old troll wife alone. "Mercy me!" she thought to herself as she saw him coming. "Here is that terrible Olli again! Whatever shall I do? I mustn't let him off this time before the troll gets back! I must keep him right here with me in the house!"

So when he came in she pretended that she was tired and that her back ached and she asked him would he watch the bread in the oven while she rested a few minutes on the bed.

"Certainly I will," Olli said.

So the old troll wife lay down on the bed and Olli sat quietly in front of the oven. The troll wife really was tired and before she knew it she fell asleep.

"Ha!" thought Olli. "Here's my chance!"

Without disturbing the troll wife he reached under the bed, pulled out the big money bag full of silver pieces, threw it over his shoulder and hurried home.

He was measuring the money when he heard the troll hallooing across to him, "Olli! Oh, Olli, are you there?"

"Yes," Olli shouted back. "I'm here! What do you want?"

"Olli, have you got my money bag?"

"Yes, I've got your money bag, but it's my money bag now!"

A few days later Olli said, "Did you know, Father, that the troll has a beautiful coverlet woven of silk and gold. I think I'll go over and get it."

His father as usual protested, but Olli laughed at him merrily and went. He took with him an auger and a can of water. He hid until it was dark, then climbed the roof of the troll's house and bored a hole right over the bed. When the troll and his wife went to sleep he sprinkled some water on the coverlet and on their faces. The troll woke with a start, "I'm wet," he said, "and the bed's wet, too!"

The old troll wife got up to change the covers. "The roof must be leaking," she said. "It never leaked before. I suppose it was the last wind."

She threw the wet coverlet up over the rafters to dry and put other covers on the bed.

When she and the troll were asleep again, Olli made the hole a little bigger, reached in his hand, and got the coverlet from the rafters.

The next morning the troll hallooed across the bay, "Olli! Oh, Olli, are you there?"

"Yes," Olli shouted back, "I'm here! What do you want?"

"Have you got my coverlet woven of silk and gold?"

"Yes," Olli told him, "I've got your coverlet, but it's my coverlet now!"

A few days later Olli said, "There's still one thing in the troll's house that I think I ought to get. It's a golden bell. If I get that golden bell then there will be nothing left that had better belong to an honest Finn."

So he went again to the troll's house, taking with him a saw and an auger. He hid until night and, when the troll and his wife were asleep, he cut a hole through the side of the house through which he reached in his hand to get the bell. At the touch of his hand the bell tinkled and woke the troll. The troll jumped out of bed and grabbed Olli's hand.

"Ha, ha!" he cried. "I've got you now and this time you won't get away!"

Olli didn't try to get away! He made no resistance while the troll dragged him into the house.

"We'll eat him—that's what we'll do!" the troll said to his wife. "Heat the oven at once and we'll roast him!"

So the troll wife built a roaring fire in the oven.

"He'll make a fine roast!" the troll said, pinching Olli's arms and legs. "I think we ought to invite the other troll folk to come and help us eat him up. Suppose I just go over the mountain and gather them in. You can manage here without me. As soon as the oven is well heated just take Olli and slip him in and close the door; by the time we come he'll be done."

"Very well," the troll wife said, "but don't be too long! He's young and tender and will roast quickly!"

So the troll went out to invite the other mountain trolls to the feast and Olli was left alone with the troll wife.

When the oven was well heated she raked out the coals and said to Olli, "Now, then, my boy, sit down in front of the oven with your back to the opening and I'll push you in nicely."

Olli pretended he didn't quite understand. He sat down first one way and then another, spreading himself out so large that he was too big for the oven door.

"Not that way!" the troll wife kept saying. "Hunch up a little, straight in front of the door!"

"You show me how," Olli begged.

So the old troll wife sat down before the oven directly in front of the opening, and she hunched herself up very compactly with her chin on her knees and her arms around her legs.

"Oh, that way!" Olli said. "I understand now; you can just take hold of me and push me in and shut the door!" And as he spoke he took hold of her and pushed her in and slammed the door! And that was the end of the old troll wife.

Olli let her roast in the oven till she was done to a turn. Then he took her out and put her on the table all ready for the feast. Then he filled a sack with straw and dressed the sack up in some of the old troll wife's clothes. He threw the dressed-up sack on the bed and, just to glance at it, you'd suppose it was the troll wife asleep.

Then Olli took the golden bell and went home.

Well, presently the troll and all the troll folk from over the mountain came trooping in.

"Yum, yum! It certainly smells good!" they said as they got their first whiff from the big roast on the table.

"See!" the troll said, pointing to the bed. "The old woman's asleep. Well, let her sleep. She's tired. We'll just sit down without her!"

So they set to and feasted and feasted.

"Ha! Ha!" said the troll. "This is the way to serve a troublesome young Finn!"

Just then his knife struck something hard and he looked down to see what it was. "Mercy me!" he cried. "If here isn't one of the old woman's beads! What can that mean? You don't suppose the roast is not Olli after all, but the old woman! No, no! It can't be!" He got up and went over to the bed. Then he came back shaking his head sadly. "My friends," he said, "we've been eating the old woman! However, we've eaten so much of her that I suppose we might as well finish her!"

So the troll folk sat all night feasting and drinking.

At dawn the troll went down to the water and hallooed across, "Olli! Oh, Olli, are you there?"

Olli, who was safely home, shouted back, "Yes, I'm here! What do you want?"

"Have you got my golden bell?"

"Yes, I've got your golden bell, but it's my golden bell now!"

"One more thing, Olli, did you roast my old woman?"

"Your old woman?" Olli echoed. "Look! Is that she?"

Olli pointed at the rising sun which was coming up behind the troll. The troll turned and looked. He looked straight at the sun and then, of course, he burst!

So that was the end of him!

Well, after that no other troll ever dared settle on that side of the mountain. They were all too afraid of the Terrible Olli!

THE NORTHERN FROG

Once upon a time, as old people relate, there existed a horrible monster which came from the barren lands to the north. It killed everything in its path, both men and animals, and if nobody had been able to stop its progress, it might have gradually swept all living things from the earth.

It had a body like an ox and legs like a frog; that is to say, two short ones in front and two long ones behind. Its tail was ten fathoms long. It moved like a frog, clearing two miles at every bound. Fortunately, it remained for several years on the spot where it had landed, and did not move farther till it had eaten the whole neighborhood bare. Its body was entirely encased in scales harder than stone or bronze, so that nothing could injure it. Its two large eyes shone like the brightest tapers both by day and night, and whoever had the misfortune to meet their glare fell under the monster's spell and was forced to throw himself into the jaws of the beast.

So it happened that men and animals offered themselves to be devoured without the Northern Frog ever moving from its place. The neighboring kings posted magnificent rewards to any-one who could destroy the monster by magic, or otherwise. Many people had tried their fortune, but their efforts were all futile. Most ended up as a tasty snack.

On one occasion, a large forest in which the monster was skulking was set on fire. The wood was destroyed, but the terri-ble monster was not harmed in the least. It was reported among old people that nobody could overcome the monster except with the help of King Solomon's Seal-Ring, on which a secret inscrip-tion was engraved. The inscription told, among other things, how the monster might be destroyed. But nobody could tell where the ring was now concealed, nor where to find a sorcerer who could read the inscription.

One day a young man, whose head and heart were in the right place, determined to set out in search of the seal-ring, trusting in his good fortune. He started in the direction of the east, where it was supposed that the wisdom of the ancients is to be sought for. After some years he met with a wise and powerful magician, and asked him for advice. The sorcerer answered, "Men have but little wisdom, and here it can avail you nothing; but God's birds will be your best guides under heaven, if you will learn their language. I can help you with it if you stay with me a few days."

The young man thankfully accepted this friendly offer, and replied, "I am unable to offer you anything in return for your kindness. But if I should succeed in my quest, I will richly reward you for your trouble." The sorcerer prepared a powerful charm by boiling nine kinds of magic herbs which he had gathered secretly by moonlight. He made the young man drink a spoonful every day, and it had the effect of making the language of birds intelligible to him. When he departed, the sorcerer said, "If you should have the good luck to find and get possession of Solomon's Seal, come back to me so that I may read you the inscription on the ring, for there is no one else alive who can do so."

The next day the young man found the world quite transformed. He no longer went anywhere alone, but found company everywhere, for he now understood the language of birds, and thus many secrets were revealed to him which human wisdom would have been unable to discover. Nevertheless, some time passed before he could learn anything about the ring. At length one evening, when he was exhausted, he lay down under a tree in a wood to eat his supper, and he heard two strange birds with bright-colored plumage talking about him in the branches.

"I know that silly wanderer under the tree," one of them said; "he has traveled far and wide without finding a trace of what he wants. He is searching for the lost ring of King Solomon."

The other bird replied, "I think he should seek the help of the Witch Maiden. She would certainly be able to help him to find it, if anyone can. Even if she herself does not possess the ring, she must know well enough who owns it now."

The first bird replied, "It may be as you say, but where can he find the Witch Maiden? She has no fixed abode, and is here today and there tomorrow. He might as well try to capture the wind."

"I can't say exactly where she is at present," said the other bird, "but in three days' time she will come to the spring to wash her face, as is her custom every month on the night of the full moon, so that the bloom of youth never disappears from her cheeks, and her face never wrinkles with age."

The first bird responded, "Well, the spring is not far off, shall we amuse ourselves by watching her proceedings?"

"Willingly," chuckled the other bird.

The young man resolved at once to follow the birds and visit the spring, but two difficulties troubled him. In the first place, he feared he might be asleep when the birds set out, and secondly, he had no wings with which he could follow close behind them. He was too weary to lie awake all night, for he could not keep his eyes open, but his anxiety prevented him from sleeping quietly, and he often woke up for fear of missing the departure of the birds. He was very glad when he looked up in the tree at sunrise and saw the bright-colored birds sitting motionless with their heads under their wings. He swallowed his breakfast and waited for the birds to wake up. However, they did not seem willing to go anywhere that morning, but fluttered about as if to amuse themselves, and went in search of food, flying from one tree-top to another till evening, when they returned to roost at their old quarters.

On the second day it was just the same.

However, on the third morning one bird said to the other, "We must go to the spring today to see the Witch Maiden washing her face." They waited till noon, and then flew away toward the south. The young man's heart beat rapidly with fear because he was afraid to lose sight of his guides. But the birds did not fly farther than he could see, and perched on the summit of a tree. The young man ran after them till he was all sweaty and quite out of breath. After resting three times, the birds reached a small open glade and perched on a high tree at its edge. When the young man arrived, he saw a spring in the midst of the opening, and sat down under the tree on which the birds were perched. Then he pricked up his ears and listened to the talk of the feathered creatures.

"The sun has not set," said the first bird, "and we must wait till the moon rises and the maiden comes to the well. We will see whether she notices the young man under the tree."

The other bird replied, "Nothing escapes her eyes concerning a young man. Will this one be clever enough to escape falling into her net?"

"We will see what passes between them," returned the first bird.

Evening came, and the full moon had already risen high above the wood when the young man heard a slight rustling, and in a few moments a maiden emerged from the trees and sped across the grass to the spring so lightly that her feet hardly seemed to touch the ground. The young man saw in an instant that she was the most beautiful woman he had ever seen in his life, and he could not take his eyes from her.

She went straight to the well without taking any notice of him, raised her eyes to the moon and then fell on her knees and washed her face nine times in the spring. Each time she looked up at the moon and cried out, "Fair and round-cheeked as now thou art, may my beauty likewise endure!" Then she walked nine times 'round the spring, and each time she sang:

"Let the maiden's face not wrinkle,
  Nor her red cheeks lose their beauty;
  Though the moon should wane and dwindle,
  May my beauty grow forever,
  And my joy bloom on forever!"

She dried her face with her long hair and was about to depart when her eyes suddenly fell upon the young man who was sitting under the tree, and she turned toward him immediately. The young man stood to await her approach. The maiden drew nearer and said to him, "How dare you spy on a maiden in the moonlight! But as you are a stranger and came here by accident, I will forgive you. You must inform me truly who you are, and how you came here, where no mortal has ever before set foot."

The youth answered with much politeness, "Forgive me, fair lady, for having offended you. I didn't mean to. I've been wandering for many days and I found this nice place under the tree, and prepared to camp here for the night. Your arrival interrupted me, and I remained sitting here, thinking that I should not disturb

you if I looked on quietly."

The maiden seemed to consider the matter a moment, then she smiled and said, "Come to my house tonight. It is better to rest on cushions than on the cold moss, I should think."

The young man hesitated for a moment, uncertain whether he ought to accept her friendly invitation or to decline it. One of the birds in the tree remarked to the other, "He would be a fool if he did not accept her offer."

Perhaps the maiden knew the language of birds, for she added, "Fear nothing, my friend. I have not invited you with any ill intention, but wish you well with all my heart."

The birds called out, "Go where you are asked, but beware of giving any blood, lest you should sell your soul!"

Then the youth went with her. Not far from the spring they arrived at a beautiful garden where stood a magnificent mansion which shone in the moonlight as if the roof and walls were made of gold and silver. When the youth entered, he passed through very splendid apartments, each grander than the last; hundreds of tapers were burning in gold chandeliers, and everywhere diffused a light like that of day.

They reached a room where an elegant supper was laid out. Two chairs stood at the table, one of silver and the other of gold. The maiden sat down on the golden chair and invited the youth to take the other. White-robed damsels served up and removed the dishes, speaking not a word and trodding as softly as if on cats' feet. After supper the youth remained alone with the maiden, and they kept up a lively conversation till a woman in red garments appeared to remind them that it was bedtime.

Then the maiden showed the young man to another room where stood a silken bed with cushions of down. "I hope you like it," she said before she retired. He thought he must have gone to heaven with his living body, for he never expected to find such luxuries on earth. But afterward he could never tell whether it was the delusion of dreams or whether he actually heard voices 'round his bed crying out words that chilled his heart, "Give no blood!"

The next morning the maiden asked him whether he would not like to stay here, where the whole week was one long holiday. And as the youth did not answer immediately, she added, "I am young and fair, as you see yourself, and I am under no one's authority, and can do what I like. Until now, it never entered my head to marry, but from the moment when I saw you, other thoughts came suddenly into my mind, for you please me. If we should both be of one mind, let us wed without delay. I possess endless wealth and goods, as you may easily convince yourself at every step, and thus I can live in royal state day by day. Whatever your heart desires, I can provide for you."

The maiden's sweet words might well have turned the youth's head, but by good fortune he remembered that the birds had called her the Witch Maiden, and had warned him to give her no blood, and that he had received the same warning at night, though whether sleeping or waking he knew not. He replied, "Dear lady, do not be angry with me if I tell you candidly that marriage should not be rushed upon at racehorse speed, but requires longer consideration. Can you allow me a few days for reflection, until we are better acquainted?"

"Why not?" answered the Witch Maiden. "I am quite content that you should think on the matter for a few weeks, and set your mind at rest."

Lest the youth might grow bored, the maiden led him from one part of the magnificent house to another, and showed him all the rich storehouses and treasure chambers, thinking that it might soften his heart. All these treasures were the result of magic, for the maiden could have built such a palace with all its contents on any day and at any place with the aid of Solomon's Seal. But everything was insubstantial, for it was woven of wind and dissolved again into wind, without leaving a trace behind. The youth was not aware of this, and looked upon all the glamour as reality.

One day the maiden led him into a secret chamber where a gold casket stood on a silver table. This she showed him, and then said, "Here is the most precious of all my possessions, the like of which is not to be found in the whole world. It is a costly golden ring. If you will marry me, I will give it you for a keepsake, and it will make you the happiest of all men. But in order that the bond of our love should last forever, you must give me three drops of blood from the little finger of your left hand in exchange for the ring."

The youth turned cold when he heard her ask for blood, for he remembered that his soul was at stake. But he was crafty enough not to let her notice his emotion, and not to refuse her, but asked carelessly, "What are the properties of the ring?"

The maiden answered, "No one living has been able to fathom the whole power of this ring, and no one can completely explain the secret signs engraved upon it. But, even with the imperfect knowledge of its properties which I possess, I can perform many wonders which no other creature can accomplish."

"Such as?"

"If I put the ring on the little finger of my left hand, I can rise in the air like a bird and fly wherever I wish. If I place the ring on the ring-finger of my left hand, I become invisible to all eyes while I myself can see everything that passes around me. If I put the ring on the middle finger of my left hand, I become invulnerable to all weapons, and neither water nor fire can hurt me. If I place it on the index finger of my left hand, I can create all things which I desire; with its aid, I can build houses in a moment, or produce other objects. As long as I wear it on the thumb of my left hand, my hand remains strong enough to break down rocks and walls."

"What is that funny writing upon it?" asked the young man.

"The ring bears other secret inscriptions which, as I said before, no one has yet been able to explain. But I suppose that they contain many important secrets. In ancient times, the ring belonged to King Solomon, the wisest of kings, in whose reign lived the wisest men. At the present day it is unknown whether the ring was formed by divine power or by human hands; but it is told that an angel presented the ring to Solomon."

When the youth heard the fair one speak in this way, he knew he wanted the ring. He pretended that he could not believe what he had heard. He hoped that by this means he would induce the maiden to take the ring out of the casket to show him when he might have an opportunity of possessing himself of the talisman. Still, he did not venture to ask her plainly to show him the ring. He flattered and cajoled her, but the only thought in his mind was to get possession of the ring. At last the maiden took the key to the casket from her bosom as if to unlock it, but she changed her mind, and replaced it, saying, "There's plenty of time for that afterwards."

A few days later their conversation reverted to the magic ring, and the youth said, "In my opinion, the things which you tell me of the power of your ring are quite incredible."

"But they're true," she insisted. The maiden then opened the casket and took out the ring, which shone through her fingers like the brightest sun-ray. She placed it in jest on the middle finger of her left hand, and told the youth to take a knife and stab her with it wherever he liked, for it would not hurt her. The youth protested against the proposed experiment; but, as she insisted, he was obliged to humor her. At first he began in play, and then in earnest, to try to strike the maiden with the knife; but it seemed as if there was an invisible wall of iron between them. The blade would not pierce it, and the maiden stood before him unhurt and smiling. Then she moved the ring to her ring-finger, and in an instant she vanished from the eyes of the youth, and he could not imagine what had become of her. Suddenly she stood before him smiling, in the same place as before, holding the ring between her fingers.

"Let me try," said he. "I want to try to do these strange things with the ring."

The maiden suspected no deceit, and gave it to him.

The youth pretended he did not quite know what to do with it and asked, "On which finger must I place the ring to become invulnerable to sharp weapons?"

"On the ring-finger of the left hand," said the maiden, smiling. She took the knife herself and tried to strike him, but could not do him any harm. Then the youth took the knife from her and tried to wound himself, but he found that this, too, was impossible.

Then he asked the maiden how he could cleave stones and rocks with the ring. She took him to the enclosure where stood a block of granite a fathom high. "Now place the ring on the thumb of your left hand, and then strike the stone with your fist, and you will see the strength of your hand," said the maiden.

The youth did so, and to his amazement he saw the stone sliver into a thousand pieces under the blow. Then he thought, "He who does not seize good fortune by the horns is a fool, for when it has once flown, it never returns."

While he was still jesting about the destruction of the stone, he played with the ring, and slipped it suddenly on the ring finger of his left hand. He heard the maiden cry, "You will remain invisible to me until you take off the ring again." But this was far from the young man's thoughts. He hurried forward a few paces and then moved the ring to the little finger of his left hand, and soared into the air like a bird. When the maiden saw him flying away, she thought at first that this experiment, too, was only in jest, and cried out, "Come back, my friend! You see now that I have told you the truth!" But he did not return, and when the maiden realized his treachery, she broke out into bitter lamentations over her misfortune.

The youth did not cease his flight till he arrived, some days later, at the house of the famous sorcerer who had taught him the language of the birds. The sorcerer was greatly delighted to find that his pupil's journey had turned out so successfully. He set to work at once to read the secret inscriptions on the ring, but he spent seven weeks before he could accomplish it. He then gave the young man the following instructions how to destroy the Northern Frog, "You must have a great iron horse cast, with small wheels under each foot so that it can be moved backward and forward. You must mount this, and arm yourself with an iron spear two fathoms long, which you will only be able to wield when you wear the magic ring on the thumb of your left hand. The spear must be thick as a great birch tree in the middle, and both ends must be sharpened to a point. You must fasten two strong chains, ten fathoms long, to the middle of the spear, strong enough to hold the frog. As soon as the frog has bitten hard on the spear, and it has pierced his jaws, you must spring like the wind from the iron horse to avoid falling into the monster's throat, and must fix the ends of the chains into the ground with iron posts so firmly that no force can drag them out again. In three or four days' time the strength of the frog will be so far exhausted that you can venture to approach it. Then place Solomon's Ring on the thumb of your left hand, and beat the frog to death. But till you reach it, you must keep the ring constantly on the ring finger of your left hand, so that the monster cannot see you, or it will strike you dead with its long tail. But when you have accomplished all this, take great care not to lose the ring, nor allow anybody to deprive you of it by a trick."

Our friend thanked the sorcerer for his advice, and promised to reward him for his trouble afterwards. But the sorcerer said, "I have learned so much magic wisdom by deciphering the secret inscriptions on the ring, that I need no other profit for myself." Then they parted, and the young man hastened home, which was no longer difficult to him as he could fly like a bird wherever he wished.

He reached home in a few weeks and heard from the people that the horrible Northern Frog was already in the neighborhood, and might be expected to cross the frontier any day. The king proclaimed that if anyone could destroy the frog, he would not only give him part of his kingdom, but his daughter in marriage as well.

A few days later, the young man came before the king and declared that he hoped to destroy the monster if the king would provide him with what was necessary. The king joyfully consented.

All the most skillful craftsmen of the neighborhood were called together to construct first the iron horse, next the great spear, and lastly the iron chains—the links of which were two inches thick. When all was ready, it was found that the iron horse was so heavy that a hundred men could not move it from its place. The youth was therefore forced to move the horse by himself, with the help of his ring.

The frog was now hardly four miles away, so that a couple of bounds might carry it across the frontier. The young man reflected how he could best deal with the monster alone, for, as he was obliged to push the heavy iron horse from below, he could not mount it as the sorcerer had directed him.

A raven flew by unexpectedly and called down to the youth, "Mount upon the iron horse and set the spear against the ground, and you can then push yourself along as you would push a boat from the shore."

The young man did so, and found that he was able to proceed in this way. The monster at once opened its mouth wide, ready to receive the expected prey. A few fathoms more and the man and the iron horse were in the monster's jaws. The young man shook with horror, and his heart froze to ice, but he kept his

wits about him and thrust with all his might so that the iron spear which he held upright in his hand pierced the jaws of the monster. Then he leaped from the iron horse and sprang away like lightning as the monster clashed his teeth together. A hideous roar which was heard for many miles announced that the Northern Frog had bitten the spear fast. When the youth turned 'round, he saw one point of the spear projecting a foot above the upper jaw, and concluded that the other was firmly fixed in the lower one; but the frog had crushed the iron horse between his teeth. The young man now hastened to fasten the chains in the ground, for which strong iron posts several fathoms long had been prepared.

The death struggles of the monster lasted for three days and three nights, and when it reared itself, it struck the ground so violently with its tail that the earth was shaken for fifty miles 'round.

At length, when the monster was too weak to move its tail any longer, the young man lifted a stone with the help of his ring, which twenty men could not have moved, and beat the monster about the head with it until no further sign of life was visible.

Immeasurable was the rejoicing when the news arrived that the terrible monster was actually dead. The victor was brought to the capital with all possible respect, as if he had been a powerful king. The old king did not need to force his daughter to the marriage, for she herself desired to marry the strong man who had alone successfully accomplished what others had not been able to do with the aid of a whole army. After some days, a magnificent wedding was prepared. The festivities lasted a whole month, and all the kings of the neighboring countries assembled to thank the man who had rid the world of its worst enemy.

But amid the marriage festival and the general rejoicing it was forgotten that the monster's carcass had been left unburied, and as it was now decaying, it occasioned such a stench that no one could approach it. This gave rise to diseases of which many people died. The king's new son-in-law determined to seek help from the sorcerer of the east. This did not seem difficult to him with the aid of the ring, with which he could fly in the air like a bird.

But the proverb says that "injustice never prospers," and that "as we sow we reap." The king's son-in-law was doomed to realize the truth of this adage with his stolen ring. The Witch Maiden left no stone unturned, night or day, to discover the whereabouts of her lost ring. When she learned through her magic arts that the king's son-in-law had set out in the form of a bird to visit the sorcerer, she changed herself into an eagle, and circled the air till the bird for which she was waiting came in sight. She recognized him at once by the ring which he carried on a ribbon 'round his neck. Then the eagle swooped down upon the bird, and at the moment that she seized him in her claws she tore the ring from his neck with her beak before he could do anything to prevent her. Then the eagle descended to the earth with her prey, and they both stood together in their former human shapes.

"Now you have fallen into my hands, you rascal!" cried the Witch Maiden. "I accepted you as my lover, and you practiced deceit and theft against me! Is that my reward? You robbed me of my most precious jewel by fraud, and you hoped to pass a happy life as the king's son-in-law. But now you have turned over a new leaf. You are in my power, and you shall atone to me for all your crimes."

"Forgive me, forgive me!" said the king's son-in-law. "I know well that I have treated you very badly, but I'm truly sorry."

But the maiden answered, "Your pleadings and your repentance come too late, and nothing can help you now. I dare not overlook your offense, for that would bring me disgrace, and make me a laughing stock among the people. Twice have you sinned against me: firstly, you have despised my love, and secondly, you have stolen my ring. Now you must suffer your punishment." As she spoke she placed the ring on the thumb of her left hand, took the man on her arm like a doll, and carried him away. This time she did not take him to a magnificent palace, but to a cavern in the rocks where chains were hanging on the walls. The maiden grasped the ends of the chains and fettered the man hand and foot, so that it was impossible for him to escape, and she said in anger, "Here you will remain a prisoner till your end. I will send you food every day so that you shall not die of hunger, but you need never expect to escape." Then she left him.

The king and his daughter endured a time of terrible anxiety as weeks and weeks passed by, and the traveler neither returned nor sent any tidings. The king's daughter often dreamed that her husband was in great distress, and therefore she begged her father to assemble the sorcerers from all parts, in hopes that they might perhaps be able to give some information respecting what had happened, and how he could be rescued. All the sorcerers could say was that he was still alive, but in great distress, and they could neither discover where he was, nor how he could be found.

At length a famous sorcerer from Finland was brought to the king. He was able to tell him that his son-in-law was kept in captivity in the east, not by a human being, but by a more powerful creature.

The king sent messengers to the east to seek his lost son-in-law. Fortunately they met with the old sorcerer who had read the inscriptions on Solomon's Seal, and had thus learned wisdom which was hidden from all others. The sorcerer soon discovered what he wished to know, and said, "The man is kept prisoner by magic art in such and such a place, but you cannot release him without my help, so I must go with you myself."

They set out accordingly, and in a few days, led by the birds, they reached the cavern in the rock where the king's son-in-law had already wasted for seven years in captivity. He recognized the sorcerer immediately, but the other one did not know him, for he was so much worn and haggard.

The sorcerer loosed his chains by his magic art, took the prince home, and nursed and tended him till he had recovered sufficient strength to set out on his journey. He reached his destination on the very day that the old king died, and was chosen king. Then came days of joy after long days of suffering, and he lived happily till his end, but he never recovered the magic ring, nor has it ever since been seen by human eyes.

THE GIANT WHO HAD NO HEART IN HIS BODY

Once on a time there was a king who had seven sons, and he loved them so much that he could never bear it when they weren't at his side. When they were grown up, six were sent to find wives, but as for the youngest, his father kept him at home. The others were to bring back a princess for him.

So the king gave the six the finest clothes you ever set eyes on, so fine that the light gleamed from them a long way off, and each had his horse, which cost many, many hundred gold coins, and so they set off.

Now, when they had been to many palaces and seen many princesses, they at last they came to a king who had six daughters—such lovely king's daughters they had never seen. They fell to courting the girls, each one, and when they had got them for sweethearts, they set off home again. A pity it was, too, because they had forgotten to bring back with them a sweetheart for Anders, their youngest brother.

When they had gone a good bit on their way, they passed close by a steep hillside, like a wall, where a giant's house was. The giant was sometimes a man, and sometimes a dwarf, for he had the power to change his appearance. The giant heard the six brothers approach and came outside. This giant had the gift of the Evil Eye, and with one gaze he turned the brothers and the six princesses to stone.

The king waited and waited for his six sons to return home, but the more he waited the longer they stayed away. "I shall never be happy again," he sighed, "not until I see the return of my sons."

"Father," Anders said to him one morning, "I've been thinking to ask your leave, again, to set out and find my brothers that's what I'm thinking."

"No! Never!" cried the king. "I shall never give you leave to go, for then you would stay away too. I would live no longer, so full of sorrow would I be for the loss of my seven sons."

But Anders had set his heart upon it. "Go I will," he said. He begged and prayed so long that the king was forced to let him go. The king had no other horse to give Anders but an old broken-down jade, for his six other sons had carried off all his best steeds. Anders did not care a pin for that, however, and sprang up on his sorry old nag.

"Farewell, Father," said he. "I'll come back, never fear, and more likely than not I shall bring my six brothers back with me." And with that he rode off.

When he had ridden a while, he came to a griffin which lay in the road and flapped its wings, and was not able to get out of the way, it was so starved.

"Oh, dear friend," moaned the griffin, "give me a little morsel of food, and I'll help you again at your utmost need."

"I haven't much food," said the prince, "and I don't see how you'll ever be able to help me much. Still and all, I can spare you a little. I see you are in dire want of it."

So he gave the griffin some of the food he had brought with him.

Now, when he had gone a bit farther, he came to a brook, and in the brook lay a great salmon which had got upon a dry place. It dashed itself about, but could not get into the water again.

"Oh, dear friend, shove me out into the water again, and I'll help you at your utmost need."

"Well," said Prince Anders, "the help you can give me will not be great, I dare say, but it's a pity you should lie there and choke." And with that he tossed the fish into the stream again.

After that he went a long, long way, and there met up with a wolf which was so famished that it lay and crawled along the road on its belly.

"Dear friend, do let me have your horse," said the wolf. "I'm so hungry the wind whistles through my ribs; I've had nothing to eat these past two weeks."

"No," said Anders, shaking his head. "This will I never do. First I came to a griffin and I was forced to give him my food. Then I came to a salmon, and I had to help him into the water again. And now you will have my horse! It can't be done, that it can't, for then I should have nothing to ride on."

"Nay, dear friend, but you can help me," said the wolf, whose name was Graylegs. "You can ride upon my back, and I'll help you again in your utmost need."

"Well! The help I shall get from you will not be great, I'll be bound," said the prince. "But you may take my horse, since you are in such need."

When Graylegs had eaten the horse, Anders took the bit and put it into the wolf's jaw, and laid the saddle on his back. Now the wolf was so strong, after such a hearty meal, that he set off with the prince as if he weighed nothing. So fast Anders had never ridden before!

"When we have gone a bit farther," said Graylegs, "I'll show you to the giant's house, where your six brothers and their sweethearts can be found."

So after a while they came to it.

"See, here is the giant's house," said the wolf, "and here are your six brothers, whom the giant has turned into stone. Here, too, are their six brides, and away yonder is the door to the house, and in that house you must go."

"I dare not go in there," said Anders. "The giant will take my life surely."

"No, no!" said the wolf. "When you get inside you'll find a princess, and she'll tell you what to do to make an end of the giant. Only mind and do as she bids you!"

Well! Anders went in, but, truth to say, he was very much afraid. When he came in the giant was away, but in one of the rooms sat the princess, just as the wolf had said, and so lovely a princess Anders had never yet set eyes on.

"Oh! Heaven help you! However did you get here?" said the princess when she saw him. "It will surely be your death! No one can make an end of the giant who lives here, for he has no heart in his body!"

"Well, well!" said Anders. "Yet now that I am here, I may as well try what I can do with him; and I will see if I can't free my brothers, who are standing turned to stone like so many statues. You, too, will I try to save, that I will."

"Well, if you must try, you must try," said the princess. "And so let us see if we can't hit on a plan. Just creep under the bed in the corner, and mind and listen to what he and I talk about. But please, you must lie as still as a mouse."

Anders crept under the bed and he had scarce got well underneath it before the giant came.

"Ha!" roared the giant. "What a smell of Christian blood there is in this house!"

"Yes, I know there is," said the princess. "There came a magpie flying with a man's bone, and let it fall down the chimney. I made all the haste I could to get it out, but for all one can do, the smell doesn't go off so soon."

So the giant said no more about it, and when night came they went to bed. After they had lain awake, the princess said, "There is one thing I'd be glad to ask you about, if I only dared."

"What thing is that?" asked the giant.

"Only, where is it you keep your heart, since you don't carry it about you?"

"Ah, there's a thing you have no business asking about. But if you must know, it lies under the door-sill," said the giant.

"Ho, ho!" said Anders to himself under the bed. "Then we'll soon see if we can't find it."

The next morning the giant got up cruelly early, and strode off to the wood, but he was hardly out of the house before Anders and the princess set to work to look under the door-sill for the giant's heart. Yet the more they dug, and the more they hunted, the more they couldn't find it.

"He has balked us this time," said the princess. "Still, we'll try him once more."

So she picked all the prettiest flowers she could find, and scattered them over the door-sill, which they had lain in its right place again. When the time came for the giant to come home again, Anders crept under the bed, and not a moment too soon it was, for the giant came stomping through the door.

"Snuffle, wuff!" went the giant's nose. "My eyes and limbs, what a smell of Christian blood there is in here," said he.

"I know there is," said the princess, "for there came a magpie flying with a man's bone in his bill, and let it fall down the chimney. I made as much haste as I could to get it out, but I dare say it must be that you can still smell it."

The Man without a Heart

THE SIX BROTHERS AND THEIR BRIDES
TURNED INTO STONES BY THE OLD MAN·

The giant didn't say another word, and that was the end of the matter. A little while after, he asked, "Who was it that has strewn flowers all over the door-sill?"

"I did, of course, who else would it be?"

"Do tell. But can I ask why?"

"Ah!" said the princess, "I'm so very fond of you that I couldn't help scattering them, when I knew your heart lay under there."

"You don't say!" said the giant. "But you must know it doesn't really lay under there."

So when they went to bed again in the evening, the princess asked the giant where his heart really was.

"Well," said the giant, "if you really must know, it lies in the cupboard against the wall."

"So, so!" thought Anders. "Soon we will try to find it!"

The next morning the giant left early, and strode off to the forest and so soon was gone. Anders and the princess were off to the cupboard hunting for his heart, but the more they sought for it the less they found it."

"Well," said the princess, "we'll just have to try him once more."

So she decked out the cupboard with flowers and garlands, and when the time came for the giant to come home, Anders crept under the bed again.

Then back came the giant.

"Snuff, snuff!" went the giant's nose. "My eyes and limbs, what a smell of Christian blood is in here!"

"I know there is," said the princess, "shortly after you left there came a magpie flying with a man's bone in his bill, and let it fall down the chimney. I made all haste I could to get it out of the house again, but after all my pains, I dare say it is what you smell."

When the giant heard that, he said no more about it; but a little while after, he saw how the cupboard was all decked about with flowers and garlands. So he asked who it was that had done that. "Who can it be but myself?" laughed the princess.

"And, pray, what is the meaning of all this tomfoolery?" grumbled the giant.

"Oh, I am so fond of you I couldn't help doing it when I

knew that your heart lay there," said the princess.

"How can you be so silly as to believe any such thing?" said the giant.

"How can I help believing it, when it was you yourself that told me?"

"You're a goose," said the giant. "You will never go to where my heart is."

"Well," said the princess, "but for all that, 'twould be such a pleasure to know where it really lies."

Then the poor giant could hold out no longer, but was forced to say, "Far, far away in a lake lies an island, on that island stands a church, in that church is a well, in that well swims a duck, in that duck there is an egg, and in that egg there lies my heart. So now you really know!"

In the early morning, while it was still gray dawn, the giant strode off into the wood to do what giants do.

"I must set off, too," said Anders. "If only I knew how to find the way." He took a long, long farewell of the princess, and when he got out of the giant's door, there stood Graylegs the wolf waiting for him. Anders told him all that had happened inside the house, and said now he wished to ride to the well in the church, if he only knew the way. The wolf bade him to jump on his back, he'd soon find the right path. Away they went, till the wind whistled after them, over hedge and field, over hill and dale. After they had traveled many, many days, they came at last to the lake. The prince did not know how to get over it, but the wolf told him, "Do not be afraid, Prince Anders, just hold on!" Then he jumped into the lake with Anders on his back, and swam over to the island. They came to the church, but the church keys hung high, high up on the top of the tower, and at first the prince did not know how to get them down.

"Do you not remember that the griffin promised to help?" said the wolf.

The prince called on the griffin, and in an instant the creature came, and flew up and fetched the keys. Anders quickly unlocked the entrance and stepped inside.

When he came to the well, there lay the duck, swimming about backward and forward, just as the giant had said. So the prince stood and coaxed it and coaxed it till it came to him, and he grasped it in his hand. But just as he lifted it from the water the duck dropped the egg into the well! Anders was beside himself! How was he to get it out again?

"Well, now," said Graylegs, "you must call the salmon." So the king's son called the salmon, and the salmon came and fetched up the egg from the bottom of the well.

"Squeeze the egg," said the wolf. Anders squeezed the egg, and miles away the giant screamed out.

"Squeeze it again," said the wolf, and Anders did so. Miles away the giant screamed again.

Anders turned to the raven and said, "Tell the giant that if he will restore life again to my six brothers and their brides, whom he has turned to stone, I will spare his life." The raven gave the message and the giant agreed. When the bird returned to report that the twelve young people were human once more, Anders squeezed and squeezed the egg to pieces, and the giant burst at once.

Now, when he had made an end of the giant, Anders rode back to the giant's house, and there stood all his six brothers alive and merry with their six sweethearts beside them. Then Anders went into the hillside to ask the other princess if she would be his bride, and she agreed.

They all set off home again to the father's house, and you may fancy how glad the old king was when he saw all his seven sons come back, each with his bride. So he called a great wedding feast, and the mirth was both loud and long, and if they have not done feasting, why, they are still at it.

ANDRAS BAIVE

Once upon a time there lived in Lapland a bailiff who was so very strong and swift of foot that nobody in his native town of Vadsö could come near him. If they were running races in the summer evenings, he would always win. The people of Vadsö were very proud of their champion, and thought that there was no other like him in the world, till, by-and-by, it came to their ears that there dwelt among the mountains a Lapp, Andras Baive by name, who was said by his friends to be even stronger and swifter than the bailiff. Of course not a creature in Vadsö believed that, and the bailiff declared, "If it makes the mountaineers happy to talk such nonsense, why, let them!"

The winter was long and cold, and the thoughts of the villagers were much busier with wolves than with Andras Baive, when suddenly, on a frosty day, he made his appearance in the little town of Vadsö. The bailiff was delighted at this chance of trying his strength, and at once went out to seek Andras and to coax him into giving proof of his vigor. As he walked along his eyes fell upon a big eight-oared boat that lay upon the shore, and his face shone with pleasure. "That is the very thing," laughed he, "I will make him jump over that boat." Andras was quite ready to accept the challenge, and they soon settled the terms of the wager. "He who can jump over the boat without so much as touching it with his heel will be the winner, and would get a large sum of money as the prize," said the bailiff. So, followed by many of the villagers, the two men walked down to the sea.

An old fisherman was chosen to stand near the boat to watch that the play was fair, and to hold the stakes. Andras, as the stranger, was told to jump first. Going back to the flag which had been stuck into the sand to mark the starting place, he ran forward with his head well thrown back, and cleared the boat with a mighty bound. The lookers-on cheered him, and indeed he well deserved it, but they waited anxiously all the same to see what the bailiff would do. On he came, taller than Andras by several inches, but heavier of build. He too sprang high and well, but as he came down his heel just grazed the edge of the boat. Dead silence reigned amidst the townsfolk, but Andras only laughed and said carelessly, "Just a little too short, bailiff. Next time you must do better than that."

The bailiff turned red with anger at his rival's scornful words, and answered quickly, "Next time you will have something harder to do." And turning his back on his friends, he went sulkily home. Andras, putting the money he had earned in his pocket, went home also.

In the following spring Andras was spotted driving his reindeer along a great fjord to the west of Vadsö. A boy who had met him hastened to tell the bailiff that his enemy was only a few miles off; and the bailiff, disguising himself as a Stalo, or ogre, called his son and his dog and rowed across the fjord to the place where the boy had met Andras.

Now the mountaineer was lazily walking along the sands, thinking of the new hut he was building with the money that he had won on the day of his lucky jump. He wandered on, his eyes fixed on the sands, so that he did not see the bailiff drive his boat behind a rock. The bailiff changed himself into a heap of wreckage which floated in on the waves. A stumble over a stone recalled Andras to himself, and looking up he beheld the mass of wreckage. "Dear me! I may find some use for that!" he said, and hastened down to the sea, waiting till he could lay hold of some stray rope which might float toward him. Suddenly—he could not have told why—a nameless fear seized upon him, and he flew away from the shore as if for his life. As he ran he heard the sound of a pipe, such as only ogres of the Stalo kind are known to use; and there flashed into his mind what the bailiff had said when he jumped the boat. "Next time you will have something harder to do." So it was no wreckage after all that he had seen, but the bailiff himself.

It happened that in the long summer nights up in the mountain, where the sun never set and it was very difficult to get to sleep, Andras had spent many hours in the study of magic, and this stood him in good stead now. The instant he heard the Stalo music he changed himself into a reindeer, and in this guise he galloped like the wind for several miles. Then he stopped to take

ANDRAS BAIVE SHOOTS THE STALO

breath and find out what his enemy was doing. Nothing could he see, but to his ears the notes of a pipe floated over the plain, and ever, as he listened, it drew nearer.

A cold shiver shook Andras, and this time he changed himself into a reindeer calf, for when a reindeer calf has reached the age at which it begins to lose its hair, it is so swift that neither beast nor bird can come near him. A reindeer calf is the swiftest of all things living. Yes, but not so swift as a Stalo, as Andras found out when he stopped to rest, and heard the pipe playing!

For a moment his heart sank, and he gave himself up for dead, till he remembered that, not far off, were two little lakes joined together by a short though very broad river. In the middle of the river lay a stone that was always covered by water, except in very dry seasons, and as the winter rains had been very heavy, he felt quite sure that not even the top of it could be seen. The next minute, if anyone had been looking that way, he would have beheld a small reindeer calf speeding northward, and by-and-by giving a great spring, which landed him in the midst of the stream. But, instead of sinking to the bottom, he paused a second to steady himself. He then gave a second spring which landed him on the further shore. Andras ran on to a little hill where he sat down and began to neigh loudly, so that the Stalo might know exactly where he was.

"Ah, there you are!" cried the Stalo, appearing on the opposite bank. "For a moment I really thought I had lost you!"

"No such luck," answered Andras, shaking his head sorrowfully. By this time he had taken his own shape again.

"Well, but I don't see how I am to get to you!" said the Stalo, looking up and down.

"Jump over as I did," answered Andras, "it is quite easy."

"But I could not jump this river. I don't know how you did!" replied the Stalo.

"I should be ashamed to say such things," exclaimed Andras. "Do you mean to tell me that a jump, which the weakest Lapp boy could make nothing of, is beyond your strength?"

The Stalo grew red and angry when he heard these words, just as Andras intended. He bounded into the air and fell straight into the river. Not that that would have mattered, for he was a good swimmer, but Andras drew out the bow and arrows which every Lapp carries, and took aim at him. His aim was good, but the Stalo sprang so high into the air that the arrow flew between his feet. A second shot, directed at his forehead, fared no better, for this time the Stalo jumped so high to the other side that the arrow passed between his finger and thumb. Then Andras aimed his third arrow a little over the Stalo's head, and when he sprang up, just an instant too soon, it hit him between the ribs.

Mortally wounded as he was, the Stalo was not yet dead and managed to swim to the shore. Stretching himself on the sand, he said slowly to Andras as he died, "Promise that you will give me honorable burial, and when my body is laid in the grave go in my boat across the fjord, and take whatever you find in my house which belongs to me. My dog you must kill, but spare my son."

Then he died, and Andras sailed in his boat away across the fjord and found the dog and boy. The dog, a fierce, wicked-looking creature, he slew with one blow from his fist, for it is well-known that if a Stalo's dog licks the blood that flows from his master's wounds, the Stalo will not die. That is why no real Stalo is ever seen without his dog. But the bailiff, being only half a Stalo, had forgotten his when he went to the little lakes in search of Andras. Next, Andras put all the gold and jewels which he found in the boat into his pockets, and bidding the boy get in, pushed it off from the shore, leaving the little craft to drift as it would, while he himself ran home. With the treasures he possessed he was able to buy a great herd of reindeer; and he soon married a rich wife, whose parents would not have him as a son-in-law when he was poor, and the two lived happy forever after.

THE GALLOWS-DWARVES

Once upon a time a parson was looking for a servant who would undertake the task of tolling the church bell at midnight in addition to his other duties. Many men had already made the attempt, but whenever they went to toll the bell at night they disappeared as suddenly as if they had sunk into the ground, for the bell was not heard to toll, and the bell-ringer never came back. The parson kept the matter as quiet as possible, but the sudden disappearance of so many men could not be concealed, and he could no longer find anybody willing to enter his service.

The more the matter was talked about, the more seriously it was discussed, and there were even malicious tongues to whisper that the parson himself murdered his servants. Every Sunday the parson proclaimed from the pulpit after the sermon, "I am in want of a good servant, and offer double wages, and good keep among other things;" but for many months no one applied for the post.

However, one day the crafty Hans offered his services. He had been last in the employment of a stingy master, and the offer of good keep was therefore very attractive to him, and he was quite ready to enter on his duties at once. "Very well, my son," said the parson, "if you are armed with courage and trust in God, you may make your first trial tonight, and we will conclude our bargain tomorrow."

Hans was quite content, and went into the servants' room without troubling his head about his new employment. The parson was a miser, and was always vexed when his servants ate too much, and generally came into the room during their meals, hoping that they would eat less in his presence. He also encouraged them to drink as much as possible, thinking that the more they drank, the less they would be able to eat.

But Hans was more cunning than his master, for he emptied the jug in one swallow, saying, "That makes twice as much room for the food." The parson thought this was really the case, and no longer urged his people to drink, while Hans laughed in his sleeve at the success of his trick.

It was about eleven o'clock at night when Hans entered the church. He found the interior lighted up, and was rather surprised when he saw a numerous company who were not assembled for purposes of devotion. The people were sitting at a long table playing cards. But Hans was not a bit frightened, or, if he secretly felt a little alarm, he was cunning enough to show nothing of it. He went straight to the table and sat down with the players. One of them noticed him and said, "Friend, what business have you here?"

Hans gave him a good stare, and presently answered, "It would be better for a meddler like you to hold his tongue. If anybody here has a right to ask questions, I think I'm the man. But if I don't care to avail myself of my right, I certainly think it would be more polite of you to hold your jaw." Hans then took up the cards and began to play with the strangers as if they were his best friends. He had good luck, too, for he doubled the stakes and emptied the pockets of many of the other players.

Presently the cock crew. Midnight must have come, and in a moment the lights were extinguished and the players, with their table and benches, vanished. Hans groped about in the dark church for some time before he could find the door which led to the belfry.

When Hans had nearly reached the top of the first flight, he saw a little man without a head sitting on the top step. "O ho, my little fellow! What do you want here?" cried Hans and, without waiting for an answer, he gave him a good kick and sent him rolling down the long flight of stairs. He found the same kind of little sentinel posted on the top stair of the second, third, and fourth flights, and pitched them down one after another, so that all the bones in their bodies rattled.

At last Hans reached the bell without further hindrance. When he looked up to make sure that all was right, he saw another headless little man sitting crouched in the bell. He had loosened the clapper, and seemed to be waiting for Hans to pull the bell-rope in order to drop the heavy clapper on his head, which would certainly have killed him. "Wait a while, my little friend," cried Hans. "We haven't bargained for this. You may have seen how I rolled your little comrades downstairs without tiring their own legs! You yourself shall follow them. But because you sit the highest, you shall make the proudest journey. I'll pitch you out of the loophole, so that you'll have no wish to come back again."

As he spoke, he raised the ladder, intending to drag the little man out of the bell and fulfill his threat. The dwarf saw his danger and began to beg, "Dear brother, spare my wretched life, and I promise that neither my brothers nor I will again interfere with the bell-ringer at night. I may seem small and contemptible, but who knows whether I may not someday be able to do more for your welfare than offer you a beggar's thanks?"

"Poor little fellow!" laughed Hans. "Your ransom wouldn't be worth a gnat. But as I'm in a good humor just now, I'm willing to spare your life. But take care not to come in my way again, for I might not be inclined to trifle with you another time."

The headless dwarf gave him his humble thanks, clambered down the bell-rope like a squirrel, and bolted down the belfry stairs as if he were on fire, while Hans tolled the bell to his heart's content.

When the parson heard the bell tolling at midnight he was surprised and pleased at having at last found a servant who had withstood the ordeal.

After Hans had finished his work he went into the hayloft and lay down to sleep.

The parson was in the habit of getting up early in the morning and going to see whether his people were about their work. All were in their places except his new servant, and nobody had seen anything of him. When eleven o'clock came, and Hans still made no appearance, the parson became anxious, and began to fear that the bell-ringer had met his death like those before him. But when the rattle was used to call the workmen to dinner, Hans likewise appeared among them.

"Where have you been all morning?" asked the parson.

"I've been asleep," answered Hans, yawning.

"Asleep?" cried the parson in amazement. "You don't mean that you sleep every day till this hour?"

"I think," answered Hans, "it's clear as spring water. Nobody can serve two masters. He who works at night must sleep during the day, for night was meant for laborers to rest. If you relieve me

from tolling the bell at night, I'm quite ready to set to work at day-break. But if I have to toll the bell at night, I must sleep in the day-time, or at any rate, till midday."

After disputing over the matter for some time, they finally agreed on the following conditions: Hans was to be relieved of his nocturnal duties and was to work from sunrise to sunset. He was to be allowed to sleep for half-an-hour after nine o'clock in the morning, and for a whole hour after dinner, and was to have the whole of Sunday free. "But," said the parson, "you might some-times help with odd jobs at other times, especially in winter, when the days are short and the work would then last longer."

"Not at all," cried Hans, "for that's why the days are longer in summer. I won't do anymore work than work from sunrise to sunset on week-days, as I promised."

Some time afterward the parson was asked to attend a grand christening in town. The town was only a few hours from the par-sonage, but Hans took a bag of provisions with him.

"What's that for?" asked the parson. "We shall get to town before evening."

But Hans answered, "Who can foresee everything? Many things may happen on the road to interfere with our journey, and you know that our bargain was that I am only obliged to serve you till sunset. If the sun sets before we reach town, you'll have to finish your journey alone."

They were in the middle of the forest when the sun set. Hans stopped the horses, took up his provision bag, and jumped out of the sledge. "What are you doing, Hans? Are you mad?" asked the pastor of souls.

Hans answered quietly, "I'm going to sleep here, for the sun has set and my time of work is over." His master did his utmost to move him with alternate threats and entreaties, but it was all of no use, and at last he promised him a good present and an increase in his wages. "Are you not ashamed, Mr. Parson?" said Hans. "Would you tempt me to stray from the right way and break my agreement? All the treasures of the earth would not induce me, for you hold a man by his word, and an ox by his horns. If you want to go to town tonight, travel on alone, in God's name, for I can't go any farther with you, now that my hours of service have expired."

"But, my good Hans, my dear fellow," said the parson, "I really can't leave you here all alone by yourself. Don't you see the gallows close by, with two evil-doers hanging on it, whose souls are now burning in hell? Surely you wouldn't venture to pass the night in the neighborhood of such company?"

"Why not?" said Hans. "These gallows-birds are hanging up in the air, and I shall sleep on the ground below, so we can't interfere with each other." As he spoke he turned his back to his master and went off with his provision bag.

If the parson would not miss the christening, it was necessary for him to go to town alone. The people were much astonished to see him arrive without a coachman, but when he related his astonishing encounter with Hans, they could not make up their minds whether the master or the servant was the biggest fool of the two.

Hans cared nothing about what the people thought or said of him. He ate his supper, lit himself a pipe to warm his nose, made himself a bed under a great branching pine tree, wrapped himself in his warm rug, and went to sleep. He might have slept for some hours when he was roused by a sudden noise. It was a bright moonlight night, and close by stood two headless dwarfs, each carrying his head under his arm and exchanging angry words. Hans raised himself to look at them better, when they both cried out at once, "It is he! It is he!" One of them drew nearer to Hans' sleeping place and said, "Old friend, we have met again by a lucky chance. My bones still ache from the steps in the church tower, and I dare say you haven't forgotten the story. We'll deal with your bones now in such a fashion that you won't forget our meeting for weeks. Hi there, comrades, come on and set to work!"

A crowd of the headless dwarfs rushed together from all sides like a swarm of gnats. They were all armed with thick cudgels, bigger than themselves. The number of these little enemies threatened danger, for they struck as hard as any strong man could have done. Hans thought his last hour was come, for he could not make any defense against such a host of enemies. But by good luck another dwarf made his appearance, just as the blows were falling fastest. "Stop, stop, comrades!" he exclaimed. "This man has been my benefactor, and I owe him a debt of grat-

Hans · Fights · the · headless · Dwarfs

itude. He gave me my life when I was in his power. Although he pitched some of you downstairs, he didn't cripple any of you. The warm bath cured your broken limbs long ago, and you had better forgive him and go home."

The headless dwarfs were easily persuaded by their comrade, and went quietly away. Hans now recognized his deliverer as the dwarf who had sat in the church-bell at night. The dwarf sat down with Hans under the pine tree and said, "You laughed at me once when I said that a time might come in which I might be useful to you. That time has now arrived, and let it teach you not to despise even the smallest creature in the world."

"I thank you with all my heart," returned Hans. "My bones are almost pulverized with their blows, and I should hardly have escaped with life if you had not arrived in the very nick of time."

The headless dwarf continued, "My debt is now paid, but I will do more, and give you something to indemnify you for your thrashing. You need no longer toil in the service of a stingy parson. When you reach home tomorrow, go straight to the north corner of the church, where you will find a great stone fixed in the wall, which is not secured with mortar like the others. It is full moon on the night of the day after tomorrow. Go at midnight, and take this stone out of the wall with a lever. Under the stone you will find a great treasure which many generations have heaped together; there are gold and silver church plates, and a large amount of money, which was once concealed in time of war. Those who hid the treasure have all died more than a hundred years ago, and not a living soul knows about the matter. You must divide one-third of the money among the poor of the parish, and all the rest is yours to do with what you like." At this moment a cock crew in a distant village, and the headless dwarf vanished as if he had been wiped out.

Hans could not sleep for a long time for the pain in his limbs, and thought much of the hidden treasure, but he dropped asleep at last toward morning.

The sun was high in the heavens when his master returned from town. "Hans," said the parson, "you were a great fool not to go with me yesterday. Look here! I've had plenty to eat and drink, and got money in my pocket into the bargain." Meantime he jingled the money to vex him more.

Hans answered quietly, "Worthy Mister Parson, you have had to keep awake all night for that bit of money, but I've earned a hundred times more in my sleep."

"Show me what you earned!" cried the parson.

"Fools jingle their copecks, but wise men hide their gold."

When they reached home, Hans did his duty zealously, unharnessed and fed the horses, and then walked 'round the church till he found the stone in the wall that was not mortared.

On the first night after the full moon, when everyone else was asleep, Hans crept quietly out of the house with a pickax, wrenched out the stone with much difficulty, and found the hole with the money, just as the dwarf had described it to him. Next Sunday he divided the third part among the poor of the parish, and gave notice to the parson that he was to quit his service, and as he asked no wages for so short a time, he got his discharge without any problem. Hans traveled a long way off, bought himself a nice farm, married a young wife, and lived comfortably for many years.

The Lindworm and the Bull

Once upon a time, when pigs were swine, a young woman who lived in Tjörnelunde set out to milk her master's cows. As she went across the fields, she saw a little brindled snake creeping along the grass. She thought it was so pretty that she took it home with her, and kept it in a little box.

Every day she gave it sweet milk and other such dainties as she could get for it. After some time had passed, it grew so big that it could no longer stay in the box, but crawled after the girl wherever she went. Even when she went out to the field to milk the cows, it went with her, and drank out of the milk pail.

Her mistress did not like this, and said to the girl, "Inga, unless you take means to have that snake killed, you will live to regret it. Mark my words!"

The girl ignored her, but it was soon evident that her snake was really a young lindworm. It grew larger every day, and finally it would not be content with the milk and other tidbits it was given, but lay outside the village and ate up the cattle and whatever else it could find. The terrible monster even devoured the occasional wayward traveler.

There was in the village a wise woman who told the people to feed up a bull on sweet milk and wheat bread, and she would show them how to rid themselves of the beast. This was done, and after the bull had been reared on this for two years, it was taken outside the village to fight the lindworm. It could not hold its own with it, however, and had to be taken home for another year in order to become strong enough. In the meantime the lindworm had become so voracious that a cow or an old horse had to be driven out to it daily, otherwise it took one for itself.

When the bull was three years old, it was so big and strong that the villagers were sure it could defeat the lindworm. While the fight was in progress, the lindworm struck a stone with its tail. So hard was that strike that it left a deep furrow in it. After the bull had defeated the lindworm, it was still so full of battle

rage that with its horns it tore up a large pool, which is still to be seen to the east of the village. No one could get near the beast so it had to be shot.

Considering that the bull had done such a feat in delivering the village and killing the lindworm, the inhabitants named the place after it, and called it Tyrslund (Bull's Grove), but this has since been changed to Tjörnelunde (Thorn Groves). On a farm close by is still to be seen the stone with the mark of the lindworm's tail. The people left it as a warning to little children not to pick up any dangerous creatures.

THE LINDWORM AND THE GLAZIER

It happened once, long before your grandfather's grandfather was born, that the bodies which were laid in Aarhus Cathedral disappeared time after time, without anyone knowing what the cause of this could be.

It was eventually discovered that a lindworm had its hole under the church, and went in by night and ate the bodies of the deceased. It was also found out that it was undermining the structure of the cathedral, so that it might fall in ruins. Against this danger help was sought, but in vain. No one could be found to save the cathedral's collapse or drive the monster away.

At last there came a wandering glazier to Aarhus Cathedral. When he learned the dire straits into which the town had come, he gave his promise that he would help them.

He made for himself a casket of mirror glass with only a single opening in it, and that only large enough for him to thrust out his sword through it. He sealed himself in the chest and had it placed on the floor of the church with four wax candles on top of it, one at each corner.

Around midnight the lindworm now came creeping through the choir-passage, and on seeing the chest and beholding its own image in the glass, it believed it to be its mate, but the glazier thrust his sword through its neck and killed it at once. The poison and blood which flowed from the wound, however, were so deadly that the glazier perished in his metal chest, sacrificing his life for the Cathedral.

THE BASILISK

It is common knowledge that when mead has been kept in a barrel for twenty years without being opened, a basilisk will be formed there. Woe to the person who then opens that cask!

It once happened in Randers, which is known for the quality and diversity of its mead, that a barrel was forgotten in the cellar. When it had lain there a long time, a basilisk was produced.

First it drank the mead until there was no more left. Then it began to growl from within the wooden barrel, and the noise grew louder and louder until the folk in the house heard it. They could not understand what was the matter with the barrel, but none was willing to approach it to investigate.

A wise man lived among the people of Randers, and when he got word of the mysterious barrel, he knew what the problem was. "You must bury the barrel deep in the earth, otherwise the time will soon come when the creature will break out of his cage, and such a monster no one can overcome." They did as he advised, and since that time nothing has been heard of the basilisk. Local people, however, will tell you that when the earth rumbles and shakes it is because the monster is trying to get loose.

Tales of the Devil

The Soldier and the Devil

The devil once encountered a soldier outside of Helsinki, and said to him, "Good friend, please help me to get through the town. I can't go alone, though I should be very glad to do so, for the two-eyed dogs would surround me in every street. They attack me as soon as I enter through the gates."

"I'd be glad to help you," said the soldier, "but one can't do any business without money."

"What do you want then?" said the devil.

"Not a great deal," returned the soldier, "for you've plenty of money. If you'll fill my gauntlet, I shall be quite satisfied."

"I've as much as that in my pocket," said the devil, and filled the glove to the brim with gold coins.

The soldier seemed to think hard for a moment and said, "I really don't know where to put you. I don't have a cart to hide you in."

"There must be something you can do," said the devil.

"Wait! I know. Just creep into my knapsack. You'll be safer there than anywhere."

"That'll do! But your knapsack has three straps. Don't buckle the third, or it might be bad for me." The devil, you see, was afraid that the buckled straps would form the pattern of the cross.

"All right! Squeeze in!"

So the devil crept into the knapsack.

But the soldier was one of those people who don't keep their word as they should. As soon as the devil was in the knapsack, he buckled all three straps tight, saying, "A soldier mustn't go through the town with loose straps. Do you think that the corporal would excuse me on your account if he saw me so untidy?"

The soldier had a friend on the other side of the town who was a smith. He marched straight off to him with the devil in his knapsack, and said, "Old friend, please beat my knapsack soft on your anvil. The corporal always scolds me because he says that my knapsack is as hard and angular as a dry shoe."

"Pitch it on the anvil," said the smith, and he hammered away at the knapsack till the wool flew from the hide.

"Won't that do?" asked he after a while.

"No," said the soldier, "harder still."

And again the blows hailed on the knapsack.

"That's enough," said the soldier at last. "I'll come to you again, if it's necessary."

Then he took the knapsack on his shoulder and went back to the town, where he pitched the devil out of the knapsack in the middle of the street. The dogs began to gather round.

The devil was crushed as flat as a mushroom. He could hardly stand on his legs. It had never gone so ill with him before; but the soldier had money enough and to spare, and there was some left over for his heirs.

When the soldier died and arrived in the other world, he went to hell and knocked at the door. The devil peeped through the door to see who it was, and yelled out, "No, no, you scamp, you're not wanted here! You may go wherever you like, but you won't get in here!"

So the soldier went to heaven, and told St. Peter how it had fared with him. The good angel replied, "Stay here now, there's plenty of room for soldiers."

Since that time the devil has admitted no more soldiers into hell.

THE MOON PAINTER

When the Lord God created the whole world, He was not totally satisfied, for there wasn't enough light. In the daytime the sun followed his course through the heavens, but when he sank at evening, when the evening glow faded into twilight and all grew dark, thick darkness covered heaven and earth, until the morning redness took the dawn from the hand of the evening glow and heralded a new day. There was neither moonlight nor starlight, but darkness from sunset to sunrise.

The Creator soon saw what was needed, and knew what He had to do. He called Ilmarine the Smith-God and said, "See to it that it should be light on earth by night as well as by day." Ilmarine listened to the command, and went to his forge where he had already created the firmament. He threw in silver, and cast it into a large round ball. He covered it with thick gold, lit a bright fire inside, and ordered it to proceed on its course across the sky. Then he forged a countless array of stars, covered them thinly with gold, and fixed each in its place in the firmament.

Now began a new life for the earth. The sun had hardly set and was borne away by the evening glow when the golden moon arose from the borders of the sky, set out on his blue path, and illuminated the darkness of night just as the sun illumines the day. Around him twinkled the innumerable host of stars, and accompanied him like a king, until at length he reached the other side of the heavens. Then the stars retired to rest, the moon quitted the firmament, and the sun was conducted by the morning redness to his place, in order that he should give light to the world.

After this, ample light shone upon the earth from above both by day and by night. The face of the moon was just as clear and bright as that of the sun, and his rays diffused equal warmth. But the sun often shone so fiercely by day that no one was able to work. Thus they preferred to work under the light of the nocturnal keeper of the heavens, and all men rejoiced in the gift of the moon.

But the devil was very much annoyed at the moon, because he could not carry on his evil practices in his bright light. Whenever he went out in search of prey, he was recognized a long way off, and was driven back home in disgrace. Thus it came about that during all this time he only succeeded in bagging two souls.

So he sat day and night pondering what he could do to better his prospects. At last he summoned two of his companions, but they could not give him any good advice. So the three of them consulted together in care and trouble, but nothing feasible occurred to them. On the seventh day they had nothing left to eat, and they sat there sighing, rubbing their empty stomachs, and racking their brains with thought. At last a lucky idea occurred to the devil himself.

"Comrades," he exclaimed, "I know what we can do. We must get rid of the moon, if we want to save ourselves. If there's no moon in the sky, we shall be just as valiant heroes as before. We can carry out our great undertaking by the dim starlight."

"Shall we pull down the moon from heaven?" asked his servants.

"No," said the devil, "he is fixed too tight, and we can't get him down. We must do something more likely to succeed. The best we can do is to take tar and smear him with it till he's black. He may then run about in the sky as he pleases, but he can't give us any more trouble. The victory then rests with us, and rich booty awaits us."

The fiendish company approved of the plan of their chief, and were all anxious to get to work. But it was too late at the time, for the moon was just about to set and the sun was rising. But they worked zealously at their preparations all day till late in the evening. The devil went out and stole a barrel of tar, which he carried to his accomplices in the wood. Meantime, they had been engaged in making a long ladder in seven pieces, each piece of which measured seven fathoms. Then they procured a great bucket, and a mop of lime-tree bast, which they fastened to a long handle.

Then they waited for night, and as soon as the moon rose, the devil took the ladder and the barrel on his shoulder and ordered his two servants to follow him with the bucket and the mop. When they reached a suitable spot, they filled the bucket with tar, threw a quantity of ashes into it, and dipped in the mop. Just at this moment the moon rose from behind the wood. They hastily raised the ladder, and the devil put the bucket into the hand of one of his servants, and told him to make haste and climb up, while he stationed the other under the ladder.

Now the devil and his servant were standing under the ladder to hold it, but the servant could not bear the weight, and it began to shake. The other servant who had climbed up missed his footing on a rung of the ladder, and fell with the bucket on the devil's neck. The devil began to pant and shake himself like a bear, and swore frightfully. He paid no more attention to the ladder, and let it go, so it fell on the ground with a thundering crash, and broke into a thousand pieces.

When the devil found that his work had prospered so ill, and that he had tarred himself all over instead of the moon, he grew mad with rage and fury. He washed and scoured and scraped himself, but the tar and soot stuck to him so tight that he keeps his black color to the present day.

But although the first experiment had failed, the devil would not give up his plan. Next day he stole seven more ladders, bound them firmly together, and carried them to the edge of the wood where the moon stands lowest. In the evening, when the moon rose, the devil planted the ladder firmly on the ground, steadied it with both hands, and sent the other servant up to the moon, cautioning him to hold very tight and beware of slipping. The servant climbed up as quickly as possible with the bucket, and arrived safely at the last rung of the ladder. Just then the moon rose from behind the wood in regal splendor. Then the devil lifted up the whole ladder, and carried it hastily to the moon. What a great piece of luck! It was really just so long that its end reached the moon!

The devil's servant set to work in earnest. But it's not an easy task to stand on the top of such a ladder and to tar the moon's face over with a mop. Besides, the moon didn't stand still at one place, but went on his appointed course steadily. So the servant tied himself to the moon with a rope, and being thus secure from falling, he took the mop from the bucket, and began to blacken the moon first on the back. But the thick gilding of the pure moon would not suffer any stain. The servant painted and smeared, till the sweat ran from his forehead, until he succeeded at last, with much toil, in covering the back of the moon with tar. The devil below gazed up at the work with his mouth open, and when he saw the work half-finished he danced with joy, first on one foot, and then on the other.

When the servant had blackened the back of the moon, he worked himself 'round to the front with difficulty, so as to destroy the luster of the guardian of the heavens on that side also. He stood there at last, panted a little, and thought, when he began, that he would find the front easier to manage than the other side. But no better plan occurred to him, and he had to work in the same way as before.

Just as he was beginning his work again, the Creator woke up from a little nap. He was astonished to see that the world had become half black, though there was not a cloud in the sky. But, when He looked more sharply at the cause of the darkness, He saw the devil's servant perched on the moon, and just dipping his mop into the bucket in order to make the front of the moon as black as the back. Meantime the devil was capering for joy below the ladder, just like a he-goat.

"Those are the sort of tricks you are up to behind my back!" cried the Creator angrily. "Let the evil-doers receive the fitting reward of their offenses. You are on the moon, and there you shall stay with your bucket forever, as a warning to all who would rob the earth of its light. My light must prevail over the darkness, and the darkness must flee before it. And though you should strive against it with all your strength, you would not be able to conquer the light. This shall be made manifest to all who gaze on the moon at night, when they see the black spoiler of the moon with his utensils."

The Creator's words were fulfilled. The devil's servant still stands in the moon to this day with his bucket of tar, and for this reason the moon does not shine so brightly as formerly. He often descends into the sea to bathe, and would like to cleanse himself from his stains, but they remain with him eternally. However bright and clear he shines, his light cannot dispel the shadows which he bears, nor pierce through the black covering on his back. When he sometimes turns his back to us, we see him only as a dull opaque creature, devoid of light and luster. But he cannot bear to show us his dark side long. He soon turns his shining face to the earth again, and sheds down his bright silvery light from above; but the more he waxes, the more distinct becomes the form of his spoiler, and reminds us that light must always triumph over darkness.

THE DEVIL'S HIDE

There was once a Finnish boy who got the best of the devil. His name was Erkki. Erkki had two brothers who were, of course, older than he. They both tried their luck with the devil and got the worst of it. Then Erkki tried his luck. They were sure Erkki, too, would be worsted, but he wasn't. Here is the whole story:

One day the oldest brother said, "It's time for me to go out into the world and earn my living. You two younger ones wait here at home until you hear how I get on."

The younger boys agreed to this and the oldest brother started out. He was unable to get employment until by chance he met the devil. The devil at once offered him a place but on very strange terms.

"Come work for me," the devil said, "and I promise that you'll be comfortably housed and well fed. We'll make this bargain: the first of us who loses his temper will forfeit to the other enough of his own hide to sole a pair of boots. If I lose my temper first, you may exact from me a big patch of my hide. If you lose your temper first, I'll exact the same from you."

The oldest brother agreed to this and the devil at once took him home and set him to work. "Take this ax," he said, "and go out behind the house and chop me some firewood."

The oldest brother took the ax and went out to the woodpile.

"Chopping wood is easy enough," he thought to himself. But at the first blow he found that the ax had no edge. Try as he would he couldn't cut a single log.

"I'd be a fool to stay here and waste my time with such an ax!" he cried. So he threw down the ax and ran away thinking to escape the devil and get work somewhere else. But the devil had no intention of letting him escape. He ran after him, overtook him, and asked him what he meant leaving thus without notice.

"I don't want to work for you!" the oldest brother cried petulantly.

"Very well," the devil said, "but don't lose your temper."

"I will lose my temper!" the oldest brother declared. "The idea—expecting me to cut wood with such an ax!"

"Well," the devil remarked, "since you insist on losing your temper, you'll have to forfeit me enough of your hide to sole a pair of boots. That was our bargain!"

The oldest brother howled and protested, but to no purpose. The devil was firm. He took out a long knife and slit enough of the oldest brother's hide to sole a pair of big boots.

"Now then, my boy," he said, "now you may go."

The oldest brother went limping home complaining bitterly at the hard fate that had befallen him. "I'm tired and sick," he told his brothers, "and I'm going to stay home and rest. One of you will have to go out and get work."

The second brother at once said that he'd be delighted to try his luck in the world. So he started out and he had exactly the same experience. At first he could get no work, then he met the devil and the devil made exactly the same bargain with him that he had made with the oldest brother. He took the second brother home with him, gave him the same dull ax, and sent him out to the woodpile. After the first stroke the second brother threw down the ax in disgust and tried to run off, and the devil, of course, wouldn't let him go until he, too, had submitted to the loss of a great patch of his hide. So it was no time at all before the second brother came limping home complaining bitterly at fate.

"What ails you two?" Erkki said.

"You go out into the cruel world and hunt work," they told him, "and you'll find out soon enough what ails us! And when you do find out you needn't come limping home expecting sympathy from us for you won't get it!"

So the very next day Erkki started out, leaving his brothers at home nursing their sore backs and their injured feelings.

Well, Erkki had exactly the same experience. At first he could get work nowhere, then later he met the devil and went into his employ on exactly the same terms as his brothers.

The devil handed him the same dull ax and sent him out to the woodpile. At the first blow Erkki knew that the ax had lost its edge and would never cut a single log. But instead of being discouraged and losing his temper, he only laughed.

"I suppose the devil thinks I'll lose my hide over a trifle like this!" he said. "Well, I just won't!"

He dropped the ax and, going over to the woodpile, began pulling it down. Under all the logs he found the devil's cat. It was an evil-looking creature with a gray head.

"Ha!" thought Erkki. "I bet anything you've got something to do with this!"

He raised the dull ax and with one blow cut off the evil creature's head. Sure enough the ax instantly recovered its edge, and after that Erkki had no trouble at all in chopping as much firewood as the devil wanted.

That night at supper the devil said, "Well, Erkki, did you finish the work I gave you?"

"Yes, master, I've chopped all that wood."

The devil was, of course, surprised, "Really?"

"Yes, master. You can go out and see for yourself."

"Then you found something in the woodpile, didn't you?"

"Nothing but an awful-looking old cat."

The devil started, "Did you do anything to that cat?"

"I only chopped its head off and threw it away."

"What?!?" the devil cried angrily. "Didn't you know that was my cat!"

"There now, master," Erkki said soothingly, "you're not going to lose your temper over a little thing like a dead cat, are you? Don't forget our bargain."

The devil swallowed his anger and murmured, "No, I'm not going to lose my temper but I must say that was no way to treat my cat."

The next day the devil ordered Erkki to go out into the forest and bring home some logs on the ox sledge. "My black dog will go with you," he said, "and as you come home you're to take exactly the same course the dog takes."

Well, Erkki went out to the forest and loaded the ox sledge with logs and then drove the oxen home following the devil's black dog. As they reached the devil's house the black dog jumped through a hole in the gate. "I must follow master's orders," Erkki said to himself. So he cut up the oxen into small pieces and put them through the same hole in the gate, he chopped up the logs and pitched them through the hole, and he broke up the sledge into pieces small enough to follow the oxen and the logs. Then he crept through the hole himself.

That night at supper the devil said, "Well, Erkki, did you come home the way I told you?"

"Yes, master, I followed the black dog."

"What!" the devil cried. "Do you mean to say you brought the oxen and the sledge and the logs through the hole in the gate?"

"Yes, master, that's what I did."

"But you couldn't have!" the devil declared.

"Well, master," Erkki said, "just go out and see."

The devil went outside and when he saw the method by which Erkki had carried out his orders, he was furious. But Erkki quieted him by saying, "There now, master, you're not going to lose your temper over a trifling matter like this, are you? Remember our bargain!"

"N-n-no," the devil said, again swallowing his anger, "I'm not going to lose my temper, but I want you to understand, Erkki, that I think you've acted badly in this!"

All that evening the devil fumed and fussed about Erkki.

"We've got to get rid of that boy! That's all there is about it!" he said to his wife.

Of course, whenever Erkki was in sight, the devil tried to smile and look pleasant, but as soon as Erkki was gone he went back at once to his grievance. He declared emphatically, "There's no living in peace and comfort with such a boy around!"

"Well," his wife said to him, "if you feel that way about it, why don't you kill him tonight when he's asleep? We could throw his body into the lake and no one would be the wiser."

"That's a fine idea!" the devil said. "Wake me up sometime after midnight and I'll do it!"

Now Erkki overheard this little plan, so that night he kept awake. When he knew from their snoring that the devil and his wife were sound asleep, he slipped over to their bed, quietly lifted the devil's wife in his arms, and without awakening her placed her gently in his own bed. Then he put on some of her clothes and laid himself down beside the devil in his wife's place.

Presently he nudged the devil awake.

"What do you want?" the devil mumbled.

"Sssst!" Erkki whispered. "Isn't it time we got up and killed

Erkki?"

"Yes," the devil answered, "it is. Come along."

They got up quietly and the devil reached down a great sword from the wall. Then they crept over to Erkki's bed and the devil with one blow cut off the head of the person who was lying there asleep.

"Now," he said, "we'll just carry out the bed and all and dump it in the lake."

So Erkki took one end of the bed and the devil the other and, stumbling and slipping in the darkness, they carried it down to the lake and pitched it in.

"That's a good job done!" the devil said with a laugh.

Then they went back to bed together and the devil fell instantly asleep.

The next morning when he got up for breakfast, there was Erkki stirring the porridge.

"How... how did you get here?" the devil asked. "I mean ... I mean where is my wife?"

"Your wife? Don't you remember," Erkki said, "you cut off her head last night and then threw her into the lake, bed and all! But no one will be the wiser!"

"W-wh-what!" the devil cried, and he was about to fly into an awful rage when Erkki restrained him by saying:

"There now, master, you're not going to lose your temper over a little thing like a wife, are you? Remember our bargain!"

So the devil was forced again to swallow his anger. "No, I'm not going to lose my temper," he said, "but I tell you frankly, Erkki, I don't think that was a nice trick for you to play on me!"

Well, the devil felt lonely not having a wife about the house, so in a few days he decided to go off wooing for a new one. "And Erkki," he said, "I expect you to keep busy while I'm gone. Here's a keg of red paint. Now get to work and have the house all blazing red by the time I get back."

"All blazing red," Erkki repeated. "Very well, master, trust me to have it blazing red by the time you get back!"

As soon as the devil was gone, Erkki set the house afire and in a short time the whole sky was lighted up with the red glow of the flames. In great fright the devil hurried back and got there in time to see the house one mass of fire.

"You see, master," Erkki said, "I've done as you told me. It looks very pretty, doesn't it, all blazing red!"

"You—you—" he began, but Erkki restrained him by saying:

"There now, master, you're not going to lose your temper over a little thing like a house afire, are you? Remember our bargain!"

The devil swallowed hard and said, "N-no, I'm not going to lose my temper, but I must say, Erkki, that I'm very much annoyed with you!"

The next day the devil wanted to go a-wooing again, and before he started he said to Erkki, "Now, no nonsense this time! While I'm gone you're to build three bridges over the lake, but they're not to be built of wood or stone or iron or earth. Do you understand?"

Erkki pretended to be frightened, "That's a pretty hard task you've given me, master!"

"Hard or easy, see that you get it done!" the devil said.

Erkki waited until the devil was gone, then he went out to the field and slaughtered all the devil's cattle. From the bones of the cattle he laid three bridges across the lake, using the skulls for one bridge, the ribs for another, and the legs and the hoofs for the third. Then when the devil got back, Erkki met him and, pointing to the bridge, said, "See, master, there they are, three bridges put together without stick, stone, iron, or bit of earth!"

When the devil found out that all his cattle had been slaughtered to give bones for the bridges, he was ready to kill Erkki, but Erkki quieted him by saying, "There now, master, you're not going to lose your temper over a little thing like the slaughter of a few cattle, are you? Remember our bargain!"

So again the devil had to swallow his anger. "No," he said, "I'm not going to lose my temper, exactly, but I just want to tell you, Erkki, that I don't think you're behaving well!"

The devil's wooing was successful and pretty soon he brought home a new wife. The new wife didn't like having Erkki about, so the devil promised he'd kill the boy. "I'll do it tonight when he's asleep," he said. Erkki overheard this and that night he put the churn in his bed under the covers, and where his head ordinarily would be, he put a big round stone. Then he himself curled up on the stove and went comfortably to sleep.

During the night the devil took his great sword from the wall and went over to Erkki's bed. His first blow hit the round stone and nicked the sword. His second blow struck sparks.

"Mercy me!" the devil thought. "He's got a mighty hard head! I better strike lower!"

With the third stroke he hit the churn a mighty blow. The hoops flew apart and the churn collapsed.

The devil went to bed chuckling to himself.

"Ha!" he said boastfully to his wife. "I got him that time!"

But the next morning when he woke up he didn't feel like laughing, for there was Erkki as lively as ever and pretending that nothing had happened.

"What!" cried the devil in amazement. "Didn't you feel anything strike you last night while you were asleep?"

"Oh, I did feel a few mosquitoes brushing my cheek," Erkki said. "Nothing else."

"Steel doesn't touch him!" the devil said to his wife. "I think I'll try fire on him."

So that night the devil told Erkki to sleep in the threshing barn. Erkki carried his cot down to the threshing floor, and then when it was dark he shifted it into the hay barn, where he slept comfortably all night.

During the night the devil set fire to the threshing barn. In the early dawn Erkki carried his cot back to the place of the threshing barn and in the morning when the devil came out the first thing he saw was Erkki unharmed and peacefully sleeping among the smoking ruins.

"Mercy me, Erkki!" he shouted, shaking him awake. "Have you been asleep all night?"

Erkki sat up and yawned.

"Yes, I've had a fine night's sleep. But I did feel a little chilly."

"Chilly!" the devil gasped.

After that the devil's one thought was to get rid of Erkki.

"That boy's getting on my nerves!" he told his wife. "I just can't stand him much longer! What are we going to do about him?"

They discussed one plan after another and at last decided that the only way they'd ever get rid of him would be to move away and leave him behind.

"I'll send him out to the forest to chop wood all day," the devil said, "and while he is gone we'll row ourselves and all our belongings out to an island and when he comes back he won't know where we've gone."

Erkki overheard this plan and the next day when they were sure he was safely at work in the forest he slipped back and hid himself in the bedclothes.

Well, when they got to the island and began unpacking their things there was Erkki in the bedclothes!

The devil's new wife complained bitterly.

"If you really loved me," she said, "you'd cut off that boy's head!"

"But I've tried to cut it off!" the devil declared. "I never can do it! Plague take such a boy! I've always known the Finns were an obstinate lot, but I must say I've never met one as bad as Erkki! He's too much for me!"

But the devil's wife kept on complaining until at last the devil promised that he would try once again to cut off Erkki's head.

"Very well," his wife said, "tonight when he's asleep I'll wake you."

Well, what with the moving and everything the wife herself was tired and as soon as she went to bed she fell asleep. That gave Erkki just the very chance he needed to try on the new wife the trick he played on the old one. Without waking her he carried her to his bed and then laid himself down in her place beside the devil. Then he woke up the devil and reminded him that he had promised to cut off Erkki's head.

The poor old devil got up and went over to Erkki's bed and of course cut off the head of his new wife.

The next morning when he found out what he had done, he was perfectly furious. "You get right out here, Erkki!" he roared. "I never want to see you again!"

"There now, master," Erkki said, "you're not going to lose your temper over a little thing like a dead wife, are you?"

"I am so going to lose my temper!" the devil shouted. "And what's more it isn't a little thing! I liked this wife, I did, and I don't know where I'll get another one I like as well! So you just clear out of here and be quick about it, too!"

"Very well, master," Erkki said, "I'll go but not until you pay me what you owe me."

"What I owe you!" bellowed the devil. "What about all you owe me for my house and my cattle and my old wife and my dear new wife and everything!"

"You've lost your temper," Erkki said, "and now you've got to pay me a patch of your hide big enough to sole a pair of boots. That was our bargain!"

The devil roared and blustered but Erkki was firm. He wouldn't budge a step until the devil had allowed him to slit a great patch of hide off his back.

That piece of devil's hide made the finest soles that a pair of boots ever had. It wore for years and years and years. In fact, Erkki is still tramping around on those same soles. The fame of them has spread all over the land and it has got so that now people stop Erkki on the highway to look at his wonderful boots soled with the devil's hide. Travelers from foreign countries are deeply interested when they hear about the boots and when they meet Erkki they question him closely.

"Tell us," they beg him, "how did you get the devil's hide in the first place?"

Erkki always laughs and makes the same answer, "I got it by not losing my temper!"

As for the devil, he's never again made a bargain like that with a Finn!

THE COMPASSIONATE SHOEMAKER

Once upon a time, when God himself was still on earth, it happened that He went to a farmhouse disguised as a beggar. A christening was taking place, and He asked the host for a lodging. But the man said, "I don't think that it's a good idea; you might easily be trodden in the confusion." The Poor Man offered to creep under the stove, and lie there quietly, but the farmer would not heed his prayer, and showed Him the door, saying "You might sleep in the mud hovel, or wherever else you like. It doesn't matter to me."

In the hovel lived a shoemaker who was always very compassionate toward the poor and needy, and would rather suffer hunger himself than allow a poor man to leave his threshold unsatisfied. God went to him and begged for a night's lodging. The shoemaker gave Him a friendly reception and something to eat, and offered Him his own bed while he himself lay on straw.

Next morning, when God took His departure, He thanked his host, and said, "I am He who has power to fulfill whatsoever the heart can desire. You have given Me a friendly and most hospitable reception and I am grateful to you from my heart, and will reward you. Speak a wish, and it shall be fulfilled."

The shoemaker answered, "Then I will wish that whenever a poor man comes to ask my aid, I may be able to give him what he most requires, and that I myself may never want for daily bread as long as I live."

"Let it be so!" answered God, who took leave of him and departed.

Meantime the people in the farmhouse were feasting and drinking, not remembering the proverbs: "a large piece strains the mouth" and "the mouth is the measure of the stomach." They set the house on fire by their recklessness, and only escaped with bare life. All their goods and chattels were reduced to ashes, and they were left without a roof to shelter them. The guests hastened home, but the farmer and his people were forced to take refuge in the shoemaker's hut. He received them in the most friendly way, and gave them clothes and shoes, and food and drink, and saw to it that they wanted for nothing till they could again provide themselves with shelter.

Besides this, needy people came every day to the shoemaker, and each received an abundant allowance.

Because he gave away all he owned, and refused no one relief, low people jeered at him, saying, "What is your object in giving everything away? You cannot make the world warm."

He answered, "We should love our neighbors as ourselves."

At length the shoemaker felt that his last hour had come. So he dressed himself neatly, took with him a staff of juniper, and set off on the way to hell. The warden trembled when he saw him, and cried out, "Throw down the staff! No one may bring such a weapon to hell." The shoemaker took no heed of this speech, but pressed on his way. At length the Prince of Hell himself met him, and cried out, "Throw down your staff and let us wrestle. If you overcome me, I will be your slave; but if I should overcome you, then you must serve me."

This did not please the shoemaker, who answered, "I will not wrestle with you, for you have such very clumsy hands, but come against me with a spear."

As the devil continued talking, and again advised him to throw away the staff, the shoemaker struck him a heavy blow with it behind the ear. Upon this, all hell shook, and the devil and his companions vanished suddenly, as lead sinks in water.

Then the shoemaker proceeded farther, and cautiously explored the interior of the underworld. In one hall lay a great book in which the souls of all children who died unbaptized were recorded. Near the book lay many keys, which opened the rooms in which the children's souls were imprisoned. So he took the keys, released the innocent captive souls, and went with them to heaven, where he was received with honor, and a thanksgiving feast was instituted in remembrance of his good deed.

SELECTED SOURCES
AND FURTHER READING

Arnason, Jøn. George E.J. Powell and Eiríkur Magnússon, Translators. *Icelandic Legends*. 1864.

Asbjørsen, Peter Christian, Moe, Jørgen. George W. Dasent, Translator. *Popular Tales from the Norse*, Edinburgh, 1888.

Asbjørnsen, Peter Christian. George W. Dasent, Translator. *Tales from the Fjeld*. Chapman and Hill, London, 1874.

Asbjørnsen, Peter Christian. H.L. Braekstad, Translator. *Round the Yule Log*. London, 1881.

Asbjørnsen, Peter Christian, Moe, Jørgen. *Eventyrbog for Børn*. Copenhagen, 1883.

Asbjørnsen, Peter Christian, Moe, Jørgen. *Udvalgte Folkeeventyr*. Kristiania, 1907.

Boucher, Alan. *Ghosts, Witchcraft, and the Other World*. Reykjavík, Iceland, 1977.

Boucher, Alan. *Elves, Trolls and Elemental Beings*. Reykjavík, Iceland, 1977.

Craigie, Alexander. *Scandinavian Folklore and Legend*. Edinburgh, 1874.

Fillmore, Parker. *Mighty Mikko*. New York, 1920.

Hofberg, Herman. W.H. Meyers, Translator. *Swedish Fairy Tales*. 1895.

Kirby, William. *The Hero of Esthonia*. London, 1895.

Lang, Andrew. *The Red Fairy Book*. London, 1890.

Lang, Andrew. *The Yellow Fairy Book*. London, 1894.

Lang, Andrew. *The Blue Fairy Book*. London, 1889.

Lie, Jonas. R. Nisbet Bain, Translator. *Weird Tales from Northern Seas*, 1893.